THE BIG GOODNIGHT

Amory Bell has a strange obsession... It began when his mother abandoned him to the care of his stern, unloving grandmother. It grew when his mother returned, years later, a wrinkled old drunk. Over the years it festers – a fanatical loathing of old age – until he is compelled to start killing the victims of his hatred. His assistants are the gullible members of a local youth movement. Boys like Oliver Mitchell, whose grandmother has just come to live in the granny-flat. Then granny is destined for ... the big goodnight.

THE BIG GOODNIGHT

by

Judy Gardiner

Dales Large Print Books
Long Preston, North Yorkshire,
BD23 4ND, England.

British Library Cataloguing in Publication Data.

Gardiner, Judy
The big goodnight.

A catalogue record of this book is
available from the British Library

ISBN   1-84262-396-6 pbk

First published in Great Britain in 1983 by Hamlyn Paperbacks

Copyright © 1983 by Judy Gardiner

Cover illustration © Anthony Monaghan

The moral right of the author has been asserted

Published in Large Print 2005 by arrangement with
Judy Gardiner, care of Rupert Crew Limited

Dales Large Print is an imprint of Library Magna Books Ltd.

Printed and bound in Great Britain by
T.J. (International) Ltd., Cornwall, PL28 8RW

For Barney Hatt,
who provided the riddles

PART ONE

Then the blue curtains parted and the box containing the earthly remains of Albert John Dansie slid smoothly between them into the dark unknown.

Staring fiercely at the toes of her shoes, his widow thought: 'Now remember, he doesn't know. He can't feel anything. What happens to him now doesn't matter.' But she kept her eyes averted until the honeyed whisper of taped organ music swelled a little and she sensed the release of tension, the putting away of handkerchiefs, in the pews behind, the curtains had closed again when she looked up and Bertie had gone – literally passed away – and then she felt her daughter take her by the forearm and lead her compassionately from the scene. One huge dry sob, more like a hiccough, burst from her but that was all.

The crematorium vicar met them at the side door, smiling kindly through gold-rimmed glasses and shaking her hand while he murmured something she was unable to catch. She smiled and thanked him, and moved on with her daughter through the red-brick cloister where, out of the wind and rain, the floral tributes were displayed. They paused dutifully to look at them. Gold chrysanthemums from Betty and Alex in Taunton; pink carnations and maidenhair fern from Cissie and Charles in Brighton; a cushion of pompom dahlias; a sheaf of yellow roses; some more chrysanthemums, and a handpicked bunch of Michaelmas daisies secured by a funnel of silver foil. Bertie's Aunt Mary, aged ninety, had sent gladioli, while Mrs Dansie's sister up in Denbighshire had sent a cross made out of some sort of heather. She would.

'It's a pity they're all so far away,' her daughter said.

'Yes,' said Mrs Dansie. 'And all so busy with their own lives.'

She meant it as a statement of fact and not as a cry of self-pity and hoped that her daughter would interpret it correctly. It occurred to her that a lot of statements made by a brand-new widow could easily be misinterpreted.

Becoming aware of the deferential shuffling of feet behind them they both turned, and Mrs Dansie drew a deep breath before holding out her hand to the first of the mourners.

There were not many. The couple with whom she and Bertie had sometimes played bridge, the woman who cleaned the house, the bank manager, a couple of friends from the golf club and the two receptionists from his surgery. She got through it by forcing herself to think of other things, like the state of the pound and the new television serial about George Sand, and they all murmured the usual well-meant platitudes, patted her shoulder and avoided her eyes.

'I think it was wise not to invite any of them back to the house,' her daughter said as they bowled through the Garden of Remembrance in the undertaker's black limousine. 'It's an awkward time of day and there's no sense in prolonging things, is there?'

Mrs Dansie agreed, and sat staring at the stubble on the back of the driver's neck.

'They don't seem to wear top hats any more, do they?'

'Who don't?'

'Undertakers. Now it's just black suits and an obsequious expression.'

'Fair enough,' said her daughter, and thought: She's seeking refuge in irrelevance, poor dear. She never used to. I wonder if it's her age or the trauma of bereavement...

'I'll be sixty next year, you know.'

'You don't look it.'

'I've got a good skin,' Mrs Dansie said vaguely.

'And you must always take care of it. Quite frankly, I haven't got much patience with people who don't take care of themselves, and by that I mean mentally as well as physically.'

'I know,' said Mrs Dansie, and when the car drew up outside her home allowed herself to be helped out by the driver. He patted her arm and murmured a condolence, but unlike the mourners looked straight into her eyes while doing so. The mark of a professional, she thought.

He then handed her a black plastic envelope embossed in gold, which he said she might care to peruse at her leisure.

'Thank you,' said Mrs Dansie, taking it. 'How kind.' She watched him reverse and drive away.

The house, a pleasant red brick one standing in a small spinney of silver birches, had a dispirited air inside. The wet autumn afternoon filled the corners with brown shadows and there had been a fall of soot in the sitting-room fireplace.

'Take your hat and coat off,' said the daughter, 'and I'll make you a cup of tea.'

'I don't really feel much like tea.'

'Coffee, then?'

'No, dear,' said Mrs Dansie with a sudden flash of animation. 'If it's all the same to you I'm going to have a large gin.'

'Fine,' said her daughter. 'But I'll have tea.' She disappeared in the direction of the kitchen.

Dear child, thought Mrs Dansie, sitting down and prodding at her hat-flattened hair. I wonder if it's good for her to be quite so thin?

Camilla Mitchell, née Dansie, had been married for three years when she set about the drastic revision of her appearance. Hitherto a tall, rather bulging girl with small eyes and a big nose, her best feature had been the cloud of shimmering fair hair she always wore loose on her shoulders. Sometimes it seemed as if she deliberately hid behind it, letting it fall like a pale silk curtain across her pudgy face and little eyes; only the nose insistently protruded, sticking its high peremptory arch through the protective covering like a rock rising from the seabed. Her father, who loved her dearly and seldom swore, was once moved to exclaim in exasperated sorrow that it wasn't so much a nose as a bloody great conk.

But apart from lovely hair she also had brains, and became a qualified architect when she was twenty-five. At twenty-seven she married a fellow architect called Seth and they set up in business in an outer London suburb. And it was when her first child, a boy called Oliver, was a year old that she decided to scrap the old Camilla and to promote an entirely new version of herself. She never said why; so far as Mrs Dansie knew the marriage was happy, she was delighted with the baby, and the firm of Mitchell and Mitchell was doing well. Perhaps that was the reason. Success demands a matching appearance, and she set about the project with all the concentrated skill she would have given to the conversion of a large house into a block of streamlined maisonettes.

She dieted and lost three stone. She joined a keep fit class, quickly changed to Yoga, and then one day arrived home from the hairdressers, with what looked like a cap of golden pile carpeting in place of the old shimmering curtain of hair that had previously shielded her. She became even thinner, with a fine-boned supple grace encouraged by the assiduous practice of Dynamic Breathing and *asanas;* her eyes sparkled like tiny jewels set above high curved cheek bones and the nose, that great disaster of a nose, was now seen as a boldly imaginative carving she carried with pride. Everyone noticed her, many with envy and all with interest, and when the transformation was complete she discarded the old name of Camilla and let it be known that henceforth she was to be called Willow. It took her father a long time to get used to the change and he made a great play of calling her Sycamore or Horse Chestnut, but her mother found it less difficult; Willow described her daughter's new lithe grace to perfection and she had always been very fond of willows anyway. Particularly the variety that wept.

Over at the table by the window Mrs

Dansie poured a thin stream of gin, added a drop or two of tonic and then raised the glass to her lips. The first sip of it made her facial muscles contort. She carried the glass over to the sofa, then reached to switch on the electric fire. There was a faint smell of singeing dust, and taking a second sip she looked round the room and resolved to buy some flowers for it. But not chrysanthemums or carnations or gladioli. And perhaps in the spring she would change the wallpaper...

Willow reappeared with a cup and saucer.

'Have some biscuits too, darling. They're in the tin.'

'No, thanks.'

No, of course not. Willow never nibbled biscuits, any more than she sipped neat gin. Smiling a little defiantly Mrs Dansie raised her glass and said 'Well, here's to widowhood.'

'Which brings us to something I want to talk to you about very seriously.' With boneless grace Willow sank down on the low chair opposite. 'Listen, Mother, Seth and I want you to come and live with us.'

'Oh, but I–' Immediate panic filled her. 'I don't think I–'

'And we decided to broach the subject directly after the funeral so that it would give you a specific project to get to grips with. There'll be a lot to think about and a lot of decisions to make, but Seth and I will be on hand to help with anything we can–'

'But where exactly?' She was calmer now, and able to play for time.

'The old stable block,' Willow said, 'over what is now the garage. It's perfect for a granny flat.'

'Yes, but–'

'The building's completely sound, and I would do the conversion plans exactly the way you wanted them. We could make it look very attractive.'

'What about council planning permission and all that?' Mrs Dansie took another sip.

'We've already got outline planning. You see, we'd never have bought the property in the first place if we hadn't been sure of it, because we always visualised being able to offer a home to you or to Father when one of you died.'

How sensible she was. How carefully calm and matter-of-fact.

'I don't know. It's all a bit soon,' Mrs Dansie said evasively. She sat staring at the red bar of the electric fire. 'But it's very kind of you both, and I feel enormously grateful.'

'There's no need for that,' Willow said briskly. 'We want to look after you because you're a very important part of our family unit.'

'Am I really?' Shocked by her own self-indulgence, Mrs Dansie quickly consoled herself with the thought that if a woman

couldn't be allowed a touch of maudlin senti-
ment on the day of her husband's funeral, it
was a poor lookout. She finished the gin and
wondered if she should pour another small
one.

'Of course you're important,' Willow said,
and reaching forward touched her on the
knee with a quick caressive hand. 'And the
gain would be on our side too, you know.
Oliver adores you.'

'*Does* he?' Mrs Dansie caught and
imprisoned her daughter's hand before she
had a chance to withdraw it. A quick vision
of Bertie's coffin sliding beyond the blue
curtains had suddenly filled her mind and
she needed a hand to hold.

'He wanted to come with me today,' Willow said. 'But a funeral's no place for a child.
In any case it was reading and comprehension at school today and this evening it's
Young Citizens.'

'Bless his heart,' Mrs Dansie said fondly.
Then she released her daughter's hand with
a pat and took her glass over to the table by
the window. She returned, bearing her own
and another one for Willow.

'Oh mother, I don't generally–'

'Neither do I,' said Mrs Dansie. 'But
today's different.'

They sipped companionably; Willow
wound her thin arms round her thin legs and
stared thoughtfully at her discarded cup of

tea while Mrs Dansie sat back on the sofa and thought of poor Bertie, of the possibility of going to live in a converted stable block, and of her nine-year-old grandson Oliver.

'Is reading and comprehension what we used to call English?'

'Yes, roughly.'

'And what are the Young Citizens?'

'Something like an updated version of the scouts and cubs. A lot of Oliver's friends belong.'

I've never heard of it, thought Mrs Dansie. Bertie and I are – were – getting a bit out of touch. Perhaps I really ought to go and live with them...

'You'd be absolutely independent of course,' Willow said, as if reading her thoughts. 'The stable block's only a few yards from the house and although we'd love to see you whenever you felt like dropping in, you'd still be your own person, if you see what I mean.'

'Yes.'

'I mean, no one would interfere with you, or keep any sort of check on your comings and goings. After all, Mother, you're not really old yet and there's no reason why you shouldn't make a new, happy life for yourself even though you've got to face the fact that it'll be without Daddy.' She hadn't called him Daddy for years.

'Yes. I know. Thank you.' The room was

growing steadily darker and Mrs Dansie switched on the second bar of the electric fire. It seared her ankles while her back remained cold, but gave a nice glow to the room.

'So will you think about it?'

'Yes, darling.'

'Promise?'

'Yes, I promise.'

'We could have a lot of fun drawing up the plans. What I would suggest as the main living-room – a sort of studio really – faces south-west and I thought about the possibility of a big double-glazed window opening onto a balcony. And if you made do with a smallish bathroom there'd be room for another bedroom for a friend to stay.'

'It sounds very nice. Perhaps Oliver would like to sleep in it sometimes.'

'Why not? It would make him feel very grown up and important.'

'I like to think of him as a friend,' Mrs Dansie said with a sudden dry choke.

'Of course he's a friend. And just think, you'd have the interest of getting to know Humphrey, too.'

'He must be nearly three months.'

'Three months next Sunday.'

'No one would ever dream you had had a baby so recently.'

'We take maternity in our stride these days,' Willow said. 'Like everything else.'

Shortly afterwards they scrambled some eggs and ate them in the kitchen. Willow asked her mother if she wouldn't prefer to lock up the house and travel back to Surrey with her for a few days, but Mrs Dansie thanked her and refused.

'I've got to get used to living alone, and the sooner I start the better.'

'You're not nervous, or anything?'

'Good God, no,' said Mrs Dansie in honest surprise. 'What's there to be nervous of at my age?'

It was a chill moonless night when she saw Willow out to the car standing close to the front door. She watched her snap the seat belt together and then clear the mist from the windscreen.

'Thank you for being such a brick, and everything,' Mrs Dansie said through the rolled down window.

'I wish I had time to do more, but in the meantime think over what we talked about,' Willow started the engine. 'I'll ring you in a couple of days.'

'But are you quite sure that Seth, for instance—'

'I'm quite sure about all of us. And especially Oliver.'

She drove away, tail lights flickering through the silver birches, and Mrs Dansie went back into the house. She gathered the glasses together and then noticed the black plastic envelope the undertaker had given her, lying in the corner of the sofa. She opened it, and found that it contained a set of short informal prayers in gothic lettering, suggestions for memorials in the form of tasteful metal plaques, stone tablets, flowering cherry trees etcetera – and the bill for Bertie's cremation with VAT included.

She dropped it on the floor and began to cry soundlessly, anguish tugging at the corners of her mouth as the reality of the situation became brutally clear for the first time. The anaesthetising shock of his death had now passed, the pathetic little busyness of notifying the authorities and of arranging the funeral was over and done with and she was alone for the first time in thirty-seven years.

She cried for quite a long while, sitting close to the electric fire and dabbing at her eyes with the handkerchief she had managed not to use during the funeral, and the only thing to comfort her was Willow's invitation to go and live close to her and the family in the stable block.

She decided to accept, and there was no means of foreseeing the horrifying outcome of her decision.

'How would you like Granny to come and live with us?'

'Here? For ever?'

'For ever, yes, but not in our house. We're

going to make her a little home of her own at the top of the stable block.'

'Oh.'

'Would you like that?'

'Yes. Be okay.'

Willow and Oliver were pushing the pram containing Humphrey round the big tangled garden. Moss covered the remains of fussy Victorian paths and ivy had threaded its way through the trees. There was a pleasant smell of damp earth and decaying leaves.

'You see, it wouldn't be much fun for poor Granny on her own, because she's beginning to get a little bit old, and when people get old they can't do all the things they used to.'

'What sort of things?'

'Run for buses, carry heavy shopping, climb up stepladders, for instance. And when they get really old they need someone to cook for them and tidy up their homes, so we thought that if Granny came to live close to us we could look after her. And I expect you'd like to help, wouldn't you?'

Oliver said he would. Then said: 'What did Grandpa die of?'

'He had a coronary thrombosis. Which is another way of saying that his heart suddenly stopped beating.'

'Did it hurt?'

'Oh no,' Willow said. 'It was just like going to sleep, really.'

'Going to sleep for ever.'

'Yes,' Willow admitted. 'I'm afraid it will be for ever.'

They turned a corner and the old stable block came into view; yellow brick and small gothic windows peering through a mesh of scarlet Virginia creeper.

'Jason Farnham at Young Citizens told Alastair that his grandmother had been run over and killed last week.'

'Oh Oliver – how awful–' Willow stopped abruptly.

'His big brother used to be in Young Citizens too, but he's gone to university now.'

'Well, we must make sure that nothing like that happens to our granny, mustn't we? That's what I mean about taking care of her. We all have to take care of everyone who belongs to us.'

'Even him.' Oliver indicated the sleeping baby.

'Certainly him, because he's far too small to take care of himself. But then you see, when he's big he'll help you take care of Daddy and me when we're old like Granny.'

'Granny'll be dead then, won't she?'

'I don't know. Sometimes old people live for a very long time.'

'Uh-huh,' said Oliver, then released the handle of Humphrey's pram. 'Can I go and play with Alastair?'

'Yes, of course. Don't forget lunch is at one.'

Gravely she watched him saunter away, hands in pockets, and then suddenly break into a gallop like a young animal scenting rain on the wind. He was brown-skinned and nimble-bodied, with a bob of straw-coloured hair surrounding agreeable features and front teeth that were temporarily a little too large. Alastair was a friend of similar age who lived four houses away.

Her husband Seth appeared, and smiled when he saw her standing there by the pram.

'Where's Oliver gone?'

'Off to find Alastair.'

He came up to her, and stood looking down at the baby. It was awake now, and they watched it move its mossy head to and fro and then screw up its face and snuffle in preparation for crying.

'It's almost his feed time.'

'Come on, old son.' Seth, a tall bearded man in well-worn but immaculate jeans, peeled back the covers and picked up the baby. It snuggled against him as he held it with tender expertise.

'Been looking at Granny's flat?'

'Yes. I think it's going to work rather well.'

'The builders are making a start next week. They phoned while you were out.'

'Good – that's great. I've just been telling Oliver that she's coming to live here.'

'Was he pleased?'

'Oh yes, very. And he was very receptive to

the idea of taking care of people, when I explained it. He seemed to grasp it intuitively.'

'He's not a bad chap.' Seth lowered his head and tickled the baby's forehead with his beard. It closed its eyes and seemed to shudder with pleasure.

'I've shown her the plans,' Willows said, 'and explained them all to her very carefully. Naturally I didn't put too much emphasis on the simple and foolproof element – after all, she's not quite sixty yet, but one's got to look ahead.'

'What did she think of the low bath?'

Willow laughed. 'She refers to it as her sunken bath and wants to know if it's going to be made out of marble. I think she saw it more in the light of Hollywood filmstar than geriatric.'

'Just as well – she's not geriatric yet.'

'No, of course not, bless her. It's just planning for the future.'

'I take it she's spending Christmas with us?'

'Yes, if that's okay–'

'Oh, naturally. I think she'll probably be at the tricky stage by then; the novelty of bereavement will have worn off and she'll just be coming to terms with the sober reality of the situation. And that's the time when it's vital to feel wanted.'

'Apart from the fact that she's my mother, I think it'll be rather fun to have a granny around. I mean, we'll all live our own lives and not interfere with one another, but she'll be in the *circle*, won't she?'

'It'll be good for the boys, too.'

The boys. They began to walk towards the house, Seth carrying Humphrey while Willow pushed the pram. A gleam of late November sunlight touched the garden with a watery green light.

'One of these days I really must learn something about gardening,' Willow said. 'Take a crash course, or something.'

'I prefer gardens to be left to their own devices, personally. Kept as a refuge for birds, children and small animals.'

They passed the ring of ash where they had celebrated bonfire night. The cruel iron stake to which the Guy Fawkes had been lashed was still in place and the remains of a charred chukka boot – one of Seth's – lay among the spent firework cases.

'What's for lunch?'

'Pizza and bean sprouts. I promised to take some drawings round to those people in Bridge Road at half past two, and Saturday's the only time they're at home.'

'I remember. Fine.'

'Will you be here to look after the boys?'

'Yes, of course. I'll give Humphrey his bottle.'

They entered the house, each glowing with a quiet and comfortable self-esteem.

'Do you think Harold would like Bertie's gold clubs?'

'Well, I don't really know. I mean – he's never *played* golf.'

'Perhaps he'd like to take it up.'

'I doubt it. So far as I know, he's never shown the slightest interest.'

'In that case, there doesn't seem a lot of point, does there?'

The two sisters stood surveying one another doubtfully, Mrs Dansie a slightly older version of Mrs Frewin, who had made the journey down from Denbighshire. Uninvited, her presence was appreciated provided it was temporary.

'It's difficult to know what to do with things like golf clubs.'

'What about Oxfam?'

'They've already had all his clothes – except his dinner jacket. I wonder if Harold–'

'Get it and let me see.'

Mrs Dansie opened the wardrobe, hung now with only her own coats and dresses except for the black barathea jacket and trousers.

'He only wore them about three times.'

'I think the sleeves might be a bit long.'

'You could have them shortened. Nothing easier – you could probably even manage it yourself.'

Mrs Frewin held the coathanger at arm's length, considering Bertie's dress clothes with a nonchalance that added to her sister's irritation.

'Don't have them if you don't want them.'

'It's not that, Celia. I'm just wondering if wearing Bertie's things mightn't make Harold feel a bit, well…'

'Creepy? Or merely pauperised?'

'Now don't start getting upset, there's a good girl. You're doing wonderfully well, but you must try not to take everything personally.' Mrs Frewin examined the trousers then laid them, with the jacket, carefully on the bed. 'It's lovely material, but the sleeves really are so amazingly long.'

'Are you hinting that there was something – *simian* about my husband?'

'No. He just had unnaturally long arms.'

'Compared to Harold, you're probably right. But poor old Harold's got such short arms, *and* legs–'

'Oh, Celia, come off it–'

'Who's that short-arsed little sod Bella's got off with? I'll always remember Father saying–'

'Father never used language like that–'

'No?'

'No. You're making it up. And if you're trying to get me rattled – well, I just won't *be* rattled. I've come down here to help and that's what I propose to do, in spite of you being cross and insulting, Celia, because I'm perfectly aware that being cross and insulting to one's nearest and dearest is all part of the emotional turmoil engendered by bereavement, particularly in the elderly–'

'Oh – *shut* up!' cried Mrs Dansie, and averting her eyes from the empty, pitifully impersonal garments that lay spreadeagled on the bed, marched from the room.

Standing by the dressing-table, her sister told herself: Count ten. Don't say or do anything until you've counted ten. And when you've counted ten remain just where you are and consider that it might be Harold, not Bertie. And then where would you be?

She looked at herself in the dressing-table mirror. She was younger than Celia, and it showed. Celia's hair was white all over except for a dark bit at the back, whereas her own still had coppery tints. Celia on the other hand was a little slimmer, but that was only due to all the sadness she had recently endured; bereavement must be really terrible, and she hoped that when the time came she and Harold could somehow contrive to go simultaneously...

She went downstairs prepared to forgive, but there was no need. Her sister had made two cups of coffee and carried them through to the breakfast room, where pearly winter sunshine illuminated the silvery wet garden. They sat in the window, gravely watching a thrush cracking open a snail shell.

'Did Father honestly call Harold a short-arsed little sod?'

'No, of course not. It was just me being rotten.'

'Oh, Celia,' Mrs Frewin said suddenly and fondly, 'are you really doing the right thing, going to live with Willow and Seth?'

Mrs Dansie stirred her coffee then slowly returned the spoon to the saucer. She appeared to be giving the question a lot of thought.

'Yes,' she said finally. 'I think I am.'

'It's not generally supposed to work, living with one's children.'

'But that's the whole point, I won't be living with them. I'll be entirely independent—'

'In that case, why not stay on here?'

'Too late now, the house is sold—'

'You sound as if you regret it.'

'No, I don't.' Mrs Dansie glanced round the room. 'I'm not enjoying the last few weeks because of the persistent feeling of saying goodbye, but I don't want to go on living here without Bertie. It's too full of the sort of memories that force themselves on me, whereas I want to remember the happiness – and there was a lot of happiness – without every room and every corner oppressing me with all the tiny details. I went to remember Bertie of my own volition, which is very different from merely being reminded of him by a lot of inanimate objects.'

'But your friends–'

'I can still keep in touch. In any case, what's wrong with making some new ones?'

'Nothing.'

They sat in silence. The thrush extracted the snail, swallowed it whole and then stood motionless, as if expecting some interior repercussion.

'When will your flat be ready?' As poor old Celia had burned her boats, the only thing now was to look on the bright side.

'In another four weeks, the builder says. I hope to move at Easter.'

'What's it like? Are you pleased with it?'

'Very. It has its own little courtyard entrance with room for my car beside the other two – one big living-room with a balcony, although I'm free to share the garden of course, and a very modern kitchen–'

'You won't be having meals with them?'

'Oh Lord, no. As I just said, I'll be completely independent.'

'I'll have to come down and see you.'

'Yes. I hope you will.'

They finished their coffee, the air heavy with thoughts unexpressed.

I never really cared for Willow, even as a child, Mrs Frewin thought. I never knew what she was thinking. And now she's so thin and extraordinary – what a pity she cut her hair off – I can't help thinking that she might upset poor old Celia's applecart with all her Yoga and funny architecture. And *Seth*. Well, he's very nice, but there's something a bit strange about a man who goes to pre-natal classes and can apparently change nappies like a woman...

Assured now that all was in order internally, the thrush flew off. Watching it, Mrs Dansie thought: I'm perfectly aware that Bella's never really cared for Willow. Even as a child she didn't like her much. But I very much doubt whether *her* daughter and son-in-law would open their hearts and their home to her in the same way if she lost her damned Harold.

'I can't help thinking how lucky I am,' she said aloud. 'For one thing, I shall see more of Oliver.'

'What's he like now?'

Without replying Mrs Dansie left the room for a moment, then returned with her handbag. She removed from it a bright yellow snapshot envelope.

'That's Oliver on the sofa, holding his baby brother.'

'What a huge Christmas tree—'

'And this one was taken on Boxing Day. Willow ... Seth ... and those are some friends.'

She passed the snapshots one by one, and the enjoyment of Christmas seemed even greater in retrospect with each moment suspended in a rich glow of better-than-life colour. Seth building Lego on the floor with Oliver; Willow in a long floating dress lighting the candles on the dining-table.

'Now that's a good one of Oliver. I got him just right.'

Mrs Frewin studied it. 'What's he wearing? Looks like some sort of uniform.'

'Yes he'd just come back from the Young Citizens' party. It's something like the Cubs – he goes once a week.'

'I've never heard of it.'

'No, neither had I, which shows how out of date we are. But nearly all Oliver's friends seem to belong, and Willow was telling me that she and Seth prefer it because one of its aims is to teach young people about ecology and the importance of not squandering the earth's resources, which I think is rather a good idea, personally.'

'Mmm.' Mrs Frewin added the snap to the others. 'Do you think he's going to have a nose like Willow?'

'If he does,' replied Mrs Dansie sharply, 'I'm perfectly certain that it'll suit him as well as it suits her.'

They put on their coats and their fur hats shortly afterwards and went for a walk. Under the birch trees the aconites had faded and a handful of crocus held their little mauve spears ready for when the sun broke through the last thin layer of cloud. At

31

the bottom of the drive the For Sale notice had been covered by a new one saying Sold.

'By the way,' Mrs Frewin said, 'I wouldn't mind having your big double bed, if you're not going to take it with you.'

'Well, I hadn't actually got as far as–'

'Oh my dear, don't let me force you. It was only an idle thought.'

'Have you thought any more about the golf clubs? And the dress suit?'

'I'll have to talk to Harold and let you know.'

They walked on, fur hats jammed down low and cold-rimmed eyes searching hungrily for further evidence of spring. There didn't seem to be any, and when they reached the end of the avenue they turned and walked back home again.

'After all,' Mrs Frewin said as her sister unlocked the front door, 'you won't actually be *needing* a double bed anymore, will you?'

'No,' said Mrs Dansie rather bleakly. 'No, I suppose not.'

'My grandmother's coming to live with us next week,' Oliver said.

Sitting on the floor of the old church hall vestibule he was changing from plimsolls into outdoor shoes. Because it had been his turn to help put away the games equipment he was the last boy to leave, and when he became aware of the Citizen Leader standing in the doorway watching him, it felt natural to make a little conversation. He liked and admired the Citizen Leader very much, but was slightly nervous of him.

'Are you pleased?'

Oliver stopped fiddling with his shoelace and said: 'Yes, I think so.'

'Is she very old?'

'Oh yes. She's got white hair.'

The Citizen Leader said nothing. He just went on standing in the doorway with his arms folded across his grey uniform shirt, watching Oliver. He was a neat pale man of no more than average height and his name was Amory Bell. From nine until five he was an electrician, but he had been involved with youth work since his late teens. He lived alone, very competently, over an old-fashioned jeweller's shop off the Bridge Road and travelled everywhere by bicycle. He had no close friends.

'When I say *old*' – it occurred to Oliver that perhaps he had been less than fair to his grandmother – 'I don't mean all feeble and daft. She likes jokes, and she can still roller-skate a bit, but you have to start her off with a shove.'

Still worrying at his shoelace, he failed to see the fleeting grimace that twitched Mr Bell's features.

'Why don't you untie them before you take your shoes off?'

'I do generally. I was in a hurry.'

'Bring it here.'

Oliver did so, and stood waiting with his hands clasped behind his back while Mr Bell picked expertly at the knot. His fingers were pale and well-tended and very strong. The knot fell apart.

'Thank you.'

'Now let's see you tie a slip reef.' He held the shoe, a scuffed brown brogue, on the palm of his hand, and waited.

Blinking in concentration Oliver took the two ends of his shoelace, began to weave them together, went wrong, and with a little cluck of nervous exasperation pulled them apart again.

'Give yourself time to think what you're doing. Left hand under, round, under again.'

He got it right.

'And what do we use slip reefs for?'

'Erm,' said Oliver. Then remembered. 'For fastening tent brailings.'

'Good.' Mr Bell gave him a tight, pale smile. 'Now undo it, put your shoe on, tie the lace in a double bow and cut off home.'

Oliver did so, crammed his uniform beret on, said goodbye and sped away. He liked and admired Mr Bell very much indeed and wished that he had had the courage to ask him what brailings were.

Running round the corner he caught up with Alastair, who was rambling along sucking sherbet from a paper bag with the aid of a bit of liquorice tubing.

'What do ghosts have for dinner?'

'Dunno.'

'Goulash.'

'Huh,' said Oliver, which was the correct reaction. In their world, jokes could be giggled at but the answers to riddles were always greeted with monosyllabic cool.

'What did the mother ghost say to the baby ghost when he was talking to his friend on the telephone?'

'Dunno.'

'Don't spook until you're spooken to.'

'Huh.'

They walked on slowly, contentedly. The dank cold of previous weeks had given way to a warm spell, with a soft south wind dropping at nightfall to give clear skies but only a hint of frost. Forsythia blazed its yellow fire in front gardens and the shops were full of Easter eggs.

'What were you so late coming out for?' Alastair finished the last of the sherbet, threw the bag away and then ate the liquorice tube with a squelching sound.

'I was talking to Mr Bell.'

'What about?'

'He asked me to tie a slip reef for him, and I did. And then we talked about my grand-mother coming.'

'He doesn't like old people.'

'Who says?'

'Everybody says. And haven't you heard about Big Goodnight?'

'No?'

'Nigel Schofield told me. His big brother told him.'

'Well, what is it?'

Alastair swallowed the last of the liquorice and squinted down his nose. 'Not telling. It's secret.'

'Bet you don't know. Bet you're just making it up.'

'Not!'

'*Are!*'

They skirmished energetically in an open gateway. Hearing them, the resident Yorkshire terrier streaked down the path and leaped furiously at their knees. It tore a triangular hole in Alastair's trousers. Gasping and giggling they fled away down the road towards their respective homes.

There was a bright naked light shining from the big new window of the stable block and Oliver approached it. The courtyard had now been cleared of builders' rubbish, although the cobbles were still yellow with swept up sand, and the freshly painted door to the granny flat stood ajar. He pushed it open and went up the stairs, inhaling the smell of putty, fresh paint and new wood.

His mother, thin as a hairpin in black trousers and polo sweater, was standing on a pair of steps painting the wall. She was whistling. Hearing him she stopped, and then turned round.

'What d'you think of this colour, Oliver?'

'S'okay.' He put his head on one side. 'But I don't like it shining.'

'It's only shining because it's wet.' She dipped the brush in the tin and recommenced work, applying the paint in long even strokes that immediately filled him with envy and admiration.

'Have a nice time at Young Citizens?'

'Uh-huh. Can I do some too?'

'Isn't it a bit late?' His parents invariably parried one question with another.

'No, not really.' He spoke without conviction.

'What about your homework?'

'Done it after tea.'

'*Did* it after tea.'

'But other boys say... Yes, well – *can* I?'

Willow sighed and glanced at her watch. 'Don't you think it would be a better idea if you had your bath – I'll be over to wash your back in ten minutes – then had your supper and read in bed for half an hour?' Her bright friendly look filled him with sudden repugnance for the grown up world.

'Okay.' He trailed back to the door. Then had an idea.

'I just wanted to help look after Granny the way you talked about. Doing things for her and making things nice because she's old and can't go up ladders and all that on her own.'

He stood there, small and patient, waiting for her reaction. He saw her lower her arm and place the brush carefully across the top of the tin, and he saw with satisfaction the bright friendly look soften to one of tender capitulation.

'You're quite right, Oliver,' she said. 'We *do* all want to share the job of making poor Granny's home nice and welcoming, don't we? And she *would* be very pleased to know that you'd done some of the painting for her – and without being asked, too. So look, nip over to the house, change into some old clothes and then you can paint the wall under the other window. I've got a smaller brush here you can have.'

He rushed down the stairs, undressing furiously as he went, and was back in time to hold the polythene bowl for her as she poured a thick smooth stream of paint into it. It looked beautiful enough to drink.

'Not too much on the brush at a time,' she said, 'and work it up and down and then across – like that.'

He took the brush from her, dipped it carefully in the bowl and began, his tongue moving backwards and forwards across his lips in rhythm with the strokes. They worked for the most part without speaking, only the

38

swish of their brushstrokes breaking the silence. Paint began to work its way down from the bristles to his fingers, sticking them to the handle. It was an agreeable sensation, and he experienced for the first time the perfect satisfaction that can only come about when pleasure and a sense of duty combine.

'Granny's going to be very happy here,' Willow remarked at length. 'Don't you think so?'

'Yes.'

'You do like Granny, don't you?'

'Yes.'

'I mean, we all know she's old, but she's very easy to get along with, and of course her being here won't make any difference to you and Humphrey and Daddy and me. We'll all still love each other just as much as ever.'

'Uh-uh.' The softness of paint oozing between fingers. The quiet joy of turning what had been a white wall into a pale green one.

'I got on with her very well when I was a little girl. Better than I did with my father, really.'

If Willow was angling for loving questions about her own childhood she was doomed to disappointment. Oliver went on painting slowly and concentratedly, the windscreen wiper tongue still beating a measured pace from one corner of his mouth to the other.

'And you see – it's a bit difficult to explain,

this – but I sort of hope my happiness in living with her and *being* with her when I was your age, will find an echo in you. She was my mother, and now she's your *grandmother.*'

'Isn't she still your mother?' Oliver didn't really mind whether she was or not. A bead of paint rolled from his fingers on to the floor; inadvertently he knelt in it.

'Of course she is, you charlie.'

Coming down from the step-ladder Willow shunted it to a fresh position before re-mounting. The wet shine had now faded from the far end of the wall, leaving it the soft matt shade she had planned as a background to her mother's furniture. She was pleased with the flat; the conversion had worked well and she planned to have pro-fessional photographs taken of it.

She had painted another sizable patch when Oliver suddenly said: 'What does Big Goodnight mean?'

'What?'

He repeated it.

'Big Goodnight? I don't know.' She turned towards him from the top of the steps, her large nose throwing its dramatic shadow on the wall. 'Where did you hear the expres-sion?'

'I can't remember.' He lied instinctively, without knowing why.

'Big Goodnight,' repeated Willow. 'It could mean anything.' Then she looked at him intently. 'No one's been trying to frighten you, have they? At school, I mean.'

He shook his head, and sensing his reluctance to discuss the matter further, she said no more. They cleaned up, passing the rag and bottle of turps from one to the other, and with the paint tins neatly stacked and the brushes soaking in a jar they left the granny flat and went back to the house.

Only the two dark words remained, hanging on the quiet air like an omen.

It was lovely. All of it was absolutely lovely, with the pale green walls dancing with sunlight, with spring flowers inclining graciously from every vase and a view across the courtyard to the house where her daughter and her son-in-law and their two little sons lived and worked and considered her with love. The kitchen was full of cupboards just the right height and the cooker had a lot of foolproof gadgets designed especially with the elderly in mind, and on the bathroom door was a clever little catch to save breaking it down in the event of her being taken ill in there.

They had thought of everything, bless them, and tears filled her eyes because she had had three sherries during the course of the housewarming and all she could think of was how thankful Bertie would be if he could look down and see how happy she was, and how lovingly intent Willow and

Seth were on the task of looking after her.

It was true that there had been moments of misgiving. In spite of telling her sister that the old home meant nothing without Bertie, during the final weeks she had found herself contemplating the coming removal to a new environment almost with terror. The pain of saying goodbye to old friends, of doing this and that for the very last time, and of seeing the house stripped bare and unexpectedly shabby brought her on more than one occasion to within an ace of phoning Willow and Seth to tell them that she couldn't come after all. Like a rabbit clinging to its burrow she clung to the familiar, and it was not until two days before the furniture van arrived that the miserable fears and apprehensions dropped away, leaving her suddenly optimistic, zestful and in total control. She banged the old front door behind her, and with a marvellously light heart climbed into her car and drove away without looking back.

The other two couples at the housewarming were neighbourhood friends of Willow and Seth; casual and charming, with open and ingenuous faces and very clean jeans and jerseys with holes in them. They sat on the floor and talked to her, admiring the flat and making her seem part of their own busy world – doctoring and teaching during the week and do-it-yourself boat-building, bread-making and body-culture at the weekends. It surprised her to learn that in spite of having large gardens they were also council allotment holders, and pursued the task of growing vegetables without benefit of chemical aid very seriously. She liked them, and marvelled at their energy.

Seth poured drinks – Willow was sipping Evian water – and passed them round with the baby hung against his chest in some sort of blue webbing contraption. It looked rather cramped and uncomfortable, (in Mrs Dansie's day babies were always laid out flat like herrings on a slab), but as Humphrey slept through the whole affair discomfort was obviously minimal.

It seemed to her a happy forecast for the future when Oliver pulled a face on being told that it was lunchtime. He and Alastair had been lying on the floor playing with a pack of cards.

'You can come back again later,' Willow said. 'If Granny will have you, that is. You mustn't be a nuisance.'

Everyone began to move towards the door, laughing and talking and thinking of Sunday beef sizzling in pre-set ovens.

'Come round and see us any time,' the two young couples told Mrs Dansie. 'We're mostly out during the week of course, but weekends we're always working around the home and we love friends to drop in.'

She thanked them and said goodbye to

43

Alastair, who muttered something unintelligible in reply.

'Now don't forget, you're really wanted,' Willow called up from the foot of the stairs. 'Feel absolutely free to come over any time you like. Even if we're busy we can always spare a moment or two – that's right, isn't it, Seth?'

'Of course it is!' The sparkle of white teeth through brown beard; the baby suspended from his neck like a symbol of virility.

She waved to them cheerily, then closed the door. The sherry's uplifting effect had worn off a little and she went through to the glittering kitchen wondering whether she could sidestep the safety precautions on the new cooker sufficiently to grill a lamb chop.

But the happy forecast regarding Oliver seemed correct when, only three days later, he came up to the granny flat and asked whether she would like to buy a ticket for the Young Citizens' concert.

'They cost twenty-five pence and you get tea and a biscuit.'

'Are Mummy and Daddy coming too?'

'No, they can't. They've got to go to a meeting about the ethnic races.'

'What a pity,' she said. Then added: 'Don't they agree with them?'

He considered. 'If they're some kind of human people I expect they do. So – can

44

you come?'

'Yes, Oliver,' she said. 'I'd love to.'

She gave him twenty-five pence from her purse, counting the coins into his small moist palm. In return he dipped into the pocket of his windcheater and drew out a typewritten duplicated ticket, which he handed to her.

She thanked him, and propped it carefully in front of the photograph of his mother, taken when she was a baby.

'Are you going to appear in the concert?'

'Yes. But only a bit.'

'I'm looking forward to it very much.'

They stood looking at one another tentatively, each waiting for the other to make the next move. They had got on very well together at Christmas, but that had been different; at Christmas there had been a lot of other people around as well, and a lot of excitement about parties and presents. Now they were on their own, and could take their time in getting to know one another below the superficial level. All they required was the impulse to do so.

'I made some coconut pyramids this morning,' Mrs Dansie said finally.

'Can I look at them?' His response was immediate.

'You can do better than that, you can eat one,' she said. 'I was just going to make myself a pot of tea.'

She did so while he hovered about the kitchen, examining things and remarking on the egg-timer cast in a block of clear plastic.

'I bought that in Cornwall when I was on holiday with my husband.'

'Grandpa?'

'That's right.' She poured the tea, and poured a glass of orange juice for him.

'Was he nice?'

He half expected her to counter the question with another one, like Don't you remember him? But she didn't. All she said was: 'Yes. Very nice.'

He ate three coconut pyramids in rapid succession.

'Tell me about the Young Citizens. What sort of things do you do there?'

Rather to her surprise he said: 'We learn to be efficient.'

'What at?'

'Everything. Right now we're doing different knots. Then we learn how to mend bicycle punctures, how to mend fuses and things, what to do if there's a fire and how to look after other children if they're ill. I know how to stop nosebleeds, now.'

'I didn't know that until I was much older than you,' she said admiringly.

'And this summer I'll be going to camp with them and we're going to learn all the different birds and animals and even the little insects, because Mr Bell says that all of

46

them and the plants and the trees are very important to the environment – like Mummy and Daddy say – and that if there's too many of *us* there won't be room for *them,* so although we've got to take care of people we've got to take care of all the others as well.'

'I absolutely agree,' Mrs Dansie said. 'I've thought for a long time now that human beings ought to stop hogging everything and give other living things a chance. Have another pyramid.'

He did so.

'Is Mr Bell the person who teaches you all these things?'

'Yes. He's our Citizen Leader and he's very good at doing everything. There's a Chief Citizen too, although he doesn't come very often because he has to go round all the other Young Citizens' places all round London and everywhere. He's a big tall man and he laughs a lot.'

'That's nice. I like people who laugh.'

'Mr Bell doesn't laugh much. But he doesn't get cross either. He seems to stay sort of the same, although–' thoughtfully Oliver licked the coconut from his fingers – 'he gets sort of very serious when he tells you about wasting the earth's resources, which means leaving bottles lying about in fields where cows can cut their feet on them and filling all the rivers up with detergent-stuff so all the fish die.'

'He sounds a very sensible man. I think it's a serious problem, too.'

'He says the trouble is we've got too many people.'

'He could well be right.'

Pouring another cup of tea Mrs Dansie wondered whether they were about to discuss birth control. Children were amazingly sophisticated these days.

'I think that what your Mr Bell is talking about is ecology,' she said. 'It's all about caring for our world as a whole, not just one section of it–'

'All the little weeny things like bees and ladybirds–'

'Exactly. They've all got their place, just like everyone else–'

'Mr Bell says humans are very greedy, and won't let go of life–'

'I think he's right. But of course–' she smiled at him over the rim of her teacup – 'some of us aren't all that bad.'

'Who?' He fell for it immediately.

'What about you and me?'

He blinked, then joined in her laughter. They both laughed quite heartily.

'Oliver,' she said. 'I like you coming to see me.'

He felt the lobes of his ears tingle with pleasure. He wanted to laugh some more, but managed to restrain himself. Sitting cross-legged on the floor he said: 'What do ghosts have for dinner?'

'I've no idea.'

'Goulash.'

Because she didn't know about the correct reaction, the cool derogatory *Huh*, she gave way to laughter again. He joined in, his big new front teeth flashing with delight.

'What did the mother ghost say to the baby ghost when he was on the telephone?'

'Don't know.'

'Don't spook until you're spooken to.'

'That's just about the most awful pun I've ever heard. What did the earwig say when it fell over the cliff?'

'Dunno.' It was such an old one that he had never heard it.

''ere we go!'

'Huh,' he said, then spoilt it by giggling. 'Can I have another coconut pyramid?'

'That'll make five.'

'They're only little ones...'

He stayed for over an hour, and when he had gone she washed his plate and glass and her own cup and saucer in the gleaming sink and then swept the coconut crumbs from the carpet with her new little sweeper.

She sat down by the big window that Willow had designed to open onto a narrow iron balcony. The neglected old trees down in the garden were starred with green buds and ringing with birdsong. Life was starting all over again, the old magic of renewal working its spell in every crevice and corner, on every humble blade of grass. She too was affected by it; her own life was beginning again, and she ran her hands over her arms. Although they sagged a little at the top – sleeveless dresses had become a thing of the past – they were still warm and strong and the hands themselves were not yet disfigured by veins. At least, not if she held them in an upright position.

She sat in the window until dusk dissolved the trees and silenced the birds, and she was filled with contentment at the thought of this Mr Bell the Citizen Leader, who was giving up his spare time in order to teach little boys like Oliver the importance of caring for all living things. Mr Bell sounded a very nice man indeed.

Mrs Krasnor shuffled from the dim secrecy of her kitchen, closing the door behind her. The door that led into the back of the shop was also closed, its glass panes obscured by a heavy lace curtain. Puffing and creaking she began to ascend the stairs, one hand hauling at the banister while the other supported a small pyrex dish covered with a white table-napkin.

It was brighter upstairs, with early evening sunlight twitching and twinkling through the ivy strands that wreathed the landing window. She stopped outside the second door, paused for a moment and then knocked. Except for the faint hissing of a lavatory cistern further down the passage there was total silence, then the door opened abruptly and Amory Bell stood there.

'Good-evening, Mrs Krasnor. Just a moment–'

He went back inside the room, moving swiftly and noiselessly, and Mrs Krasnor, whom experience had long taught never to expect an invitation to enter, slid round the doorpost and stood with her back to the bedside table, proffering the pyrex dish with a wheedling smile.

'I thought you might like a little taste of what I cooked for Poppa this morning. It's a favourite from his childhood days.'

'Thanks. Very kind, Mrs Krasnor.' Amory Bell swept up the rent book which lay on top of the small bureau. Several pound notes protruded from the inside of it. He gave it to Mrs Krasnor and accepted the dish from her, and without looking under its cover put it down on the bedside table.

'Very kind. Thank you,' he repeated. And stood waiting for her to go.

'Blinis,' said Mrs Krasnor. 'Back home in the old days rich people ate them with caviar.'

He nodded and continued to wait for her departure. She was a fat old woman with dyed black hair and prominent Pekinese eyes that glistened with kindness. She and her husband, two particles of middle European dust blown westward by the Hitler storm, had worked and saved and learned to speak English and had bought the house and shop almost twenty years ago. They had had one child, a boy who had died of typhus in one of the camps at the age of three, and although the memory of him had been almost obliterated by time – no photograph existed – they continued to refer to one another as Momma and Poppa. Both would have liked to cherish their lodger a little more; they admired his quiet, clean English self-sufficiency and were awed by the knowledge that most of his spare time was spent in voluntary work with the young.

'Thank you, Mrs Krasnor,' Amory Bell repeated. He stood holding the door.

'Are you going to work with the children again tonight?'

'The boys – yes. There's a meeting later on.'

'So. What wonderful things you do, although–' she wagged a playful finger at him, 'sometimes Poppa he says to me that young man of ours he works too hard. He takes no rest, no time for himself. He should think more of his own self and not all the time of other people.'

'I enjoy what I do.'

'Of course, of course, because you are a

good man, Mr Bell. And tonight when you come back, come and drink coffee with us. I will have it ready and hot–'

'Very kind of you, Mrs Krasnor, but I may be late tonight. There are one or two other things–'

'Of course, of course,' she nodded, her Pekinese eyes overflowing with affectionate concern, 'but it will be no trouble, and you must not be shy, Mr Bell. You must not feel shy to come in somewhere strange–'

'Thank you for the invitation, Mrs Krasnor. Perhaps another time.' Smiling with firmly closed lips he began to push the door to. It came to rest against the soft toe of Mrs Krasnor's bedroom slipper. 'So I'll say goodnight now, and thank you again for the delicious er...'

She found herself outside on the landing. Smiling and shaking her head at the marvellous altruism of Mr Bell she went back to the kitchen where Poppa, in shirtsleeves, was reading the evening paper.

'That young man of ours he works too hard and he takes life too serious.'

'He pays the rent and he stays out of trouble,' Poppa said. 'What else you want?'

'Nothing. Except...' She sat down with a sigh, then after a minute or two reached for her knitting.

Upstairs in his room Amory Bell tied his uniform tie under the collar of his grey uniform shirt and secured it in place with the League of Young Citizens badge. Sitting on the bed he put on his shoes, brown and freshly polished, and tied the laces in a double bow. It was a pleasant-looking uniform, non-assertive, non-aggressive, and he wore it with an unobtrusive neatness rather than distinction. Putting on the green battledress that matched the green trousers, he looked round his bed-sitting room to make sure that he would be leaving everything in order. The window was fastened, his two supper dishes washed and put away behind the plastic curtain, the clothes he had worn for work hung up in the wardrobe. He smoothed the bed where he had been sitting on it and then his eye fell on the pyrex bowl on the bedside table. Without examining its contents he placed it beside the small and scrupulously clean sink and then drew the plastic curtain back in place again. Putting on his uniform beret he left the room, locking the door.

His bicycle had its home in the shed at the bottom of the garden. He let himself out of the back door, passing the smell of foreign cooking and the low burble of a radio. He was aware that the Krasnors would be watching him from their window; watching him with the half-yearning, half-humorous benevolence of loving parents, and because of it he felt his spine stiffening and his pace accelerating to a hostile quick-march. He had nothing against the Krasnors provided they left him alone, and he thought with irony of Mrs Krasnor's repeated attempts to entice him into their own living quarters. Don't be shy of somewhere strange, she said, quite unaware of the fact that he knew every nook and cranny of both house and shop.

His own childhood had been a strange one, his conception an accident, and after neat whisky coupled with hot baths and jumping off bedroom chairs had failed to dislodge him his parents had braced themselves against the prospect of four months without work, for one was not able to work without the other. Frances and John Bell, known professionally as Frankie & Johnnie, were a double song-and-dance act playing the Forces' clubs and the munition factory canteens in a wartime ENSA company.

Frankie and Johnnie were lovers was the introductory music, the theme tune hammered out each time on some battered old piano while cups and saucers rattled and wolf whistles shrilled at the sight of Frankie's pink cavorting limbs and desperate smile beneath the preposterously garlanded hat. Johnnie's smile had been easier and his manner more casual because he had all the best lines.

'I love you, I love you. Your lips are like petals–'

'My lips are like petals?'

'Yeah, bicycle petals.'

A hurt pout, chin buried in a shoulder strap of wartime paper roses.

'Your teeth are like the stars above–'

'My teeth are like the stars above–'

'Yeah, they all come out at night.'

It was old, old stuff even in 1942 but they worked hard, hoping for the big break that would land them in the West End or on the BBC. Instead, they got landed with a baby.

Terrified by the thought of being called up, Johnnie got a temporary job on a hospital switchboard and one day filched a sheet of official writing paper from matron's office upon which he wrote: *This is to certify that John Henry Bell has flat feet and is therefore exempt from serving in HM Forces.* Folded inside his civilian identity card it made his mind a little easier, although the terror still lurked. He trained himself to walk slowly and clumsily with his toes splayed outwards while Frankie, alone in their furnished room, cried because she had heartburn and haemorrhoids and couldn't stand the smell of frying. Sometimes Johnnie would come home and say Christ knows how we'll get out of the mess you've got us into, then other times he would bring back a bottle of beer and after a couple of glasses would persuade Frankie to partner him in a few of the old routine dance steps. Giggling she would attempt a buck and wing with the baby bouncing under her skirt

like a pig in a sack, then she would see Johnnie's squeamish expression and lumber off to
the bedroom for another good cry.

Amory was born in September. Singapore
had fallen, so had Tobruk, but Johnnie told
Frankie that he had wangled a panto
booking for them in Grimsby, almost before
she came out of the ether.

'How long'll it take you to get your figure
back?'

'Uh?'

'I mean, can they sort of bandage you up
tight?'

'Oh Johnnie, it looks like a little bald
monkey–'

'What does?'

'The baby. The *baby* does.'

She went home too soon and the baby
screamed all night. The landlady said they
would have to look round for somewhere
else, and Johnnie left his hospital job and
told Frankie that if she didn't start limbering
up soon he'd have to look around for another partner. So she took pills to get rid of
her breast milk, had a new perm and
attended rehearsals with Amory packed in a
moses basket with her leotard and tap shoes.

The members of the new company were
either very young or very old, but they were
also very cheerful and she suddenly found
herself happy to be working again. Then,
like an extraordinary and totally unexpected

bonus, Amory smiled at her for the first time with recognition, and her reaction was like that of falling in love. In a matter of seconds he had become a real living person, and when their latest landlady offered to look after him during the long and increasingly arduous hours of rehearsal Frankie joyously refused. She could no longer bear to be parted from him, and as her skills in handling him and interpreting his needs increased, so the idea of any kind of mother substitute became increasingly abhorrent. 'I don't know how anybody *could*,' she would say. 'Not when it's their very *own*.'

Everyone in the company wanted to cuddle him, and condescending pride in the achieving of him persuaded Johnnie to refer to him as My Big Sonnyboy. On the last night of the show he was wrapped in the principal boy's cloak and carried on stage to take a curtain with the rest of the cast. He smiled toothlessly, disarmingly, and the producer held him aloft and said Ladies and Gentlemen, this is what we are fighting for. This little bundle is our hope of the future, the reason for our determination to free the world from the curse of Adolf Hitler...

Back with ENSA, Frankie and Johnnie toured bomber stations, searchlight batteries, garrison theatres and military hospitals, and they took Amory with them. He learned to walk in an improvised dressing-room on

Salisbury Plain.

He was a contented child, easily pleased and able to accept philosophically the irregular hours, the constant moving from one place to another and the tempestuous quarrels that occasionally broke out among the spangly jangly larger-than-life aunties and uncles who were temporarily a part of the show and a part of his life. There were quarrels, tears and slanging matches, but there was always someone to pick him up when he fell down, to kiss him and hug him and sing silly songs and pull funny faces to make him laugh. He loved the warmth and the laughter, the smell of sweat and make-up, and for a long while he believed his name to be Darling rather than Amory.

They all loved him and he loved them back, but never did he confuse this casual happy-go-lucky affection with the deep and almost painful adoration he reserved for his mother. He adored everything about her: her front teeth, which overlapped one another very slightly; her yellow hair that sprang back in little wiry curls no matter how hard he tried to smooth it down flat with his hands; the spiky black eyelashes, each one with a little round blob of mascara at the tip, which she used to flutter against his waiting cheek in what she called a butterfly kiss. He adored her voice with its husky cockney undertones, the warm shadow of her cleavage and the little crooked toes that were never crammed into her tap shoes without a wince of pain; and when she was on stage with his father he would toddle round the dressing-room, touching her improvised wartime costumes and hiding his face in them while he waited for the sound of applause that would bring her back, sweating and panting and already flicking buttons undone in preparation for the next quick change.

He loved her so much that sometimes it almost felt as if he *was* her, and he sobbed with what seemed to be real pain on the day she cut her finger on a piece of broken glass. His father, whom he also loved, bought him a big ginger-coloured teddy bear wearing a blue bow tie, but when he went to bed it was always with an old swansdown powderpuff belonging to his mother. He could never go to sleep unless it was clenched tight in his hand.

The war had been over for two years and his parents were appearing in a summer show at Southend-on-Sea when they told him that a nice kind gentleman had been round to see them about sending him to school.

'All big boys have to go to school,' his father said, making a bright face at him. 'You'll have lots of playmates of your own age and you'll learn all sorts of clever things and Mum and I won't half be proud of you. Won't we, Mum?'

With her face averted, Frankie said that they would.

It sounded quite nice. 'When'll I go?'

'In September. When we finish here.'

'Will you be coming too?'

No, they said. Mums and Dads don't go to school, it's only for their children. 'But if we could be little like you, we'd go back again like a shot,' added his father, and with his legs half folded beneath him and his body held perkily upright, waddled rapidly round the room.

Amory laughed and tried to imitate him. Already he could execute quite a few dance steps and was not averse to singing some of their songs in a clear high treble. He presumed that he would learn some more when he went to this mysterious place called school.

He thought about it often, sitting on the beach with his Mickey Mouse bucket and spade while his parents were working. For the first time he began to notice other children; the bigger ones shouted and ran, played cricket and ate candy-floss, and it was strange to think that he would soon become one of them. Strange, but not frightening, and so he watched the summer paintwork fade on the pier, the cockle and winkle stalls close down one by one, and then the padlocking together of all the little wooden trains and horses on the Peter Pan roundabout. The mornings were misty and the evenings sharply cold beneath the brazen swagger of the Illuminations, and then quite suddenly it was time to go.

His parents didn't tell him until the night before that they were joining a new show up in Manchester, while he was going to a place called Ilford to live with his grandmother.

'My mother and father couldn't come, so this is my grandmother,' Oliver said.

Several weeks after he had sold her the ticket, he and Mrs Dansie were filing into the church hall on the evening of the Young Citizens' concert when Amory Bell pushed his way through the crowd and came to speak to the Young Citizen who was collecting the tickets.

'Good evening.' He smiled briefly at Mrs Dansie, who smiled back and held out her hand.

'It looks as if you're going to have a full house, Mr Bell.'

'I hope so.' He turned to Oliver, and Mrs Dansie's hand remained unshaken.

'Oliver, if you're not appearing in the first item will you nip round and see if they want any help filling the tea urns?'

Delighted to be of use, Oliver disappeared.

'Being a Young Citizen seems to mean a great deal to him,' Mrs Dansie remarked pleasantly. 'He tells me quite a lot about it.'

Pushed close by the chattering surge of people she found herself examining Mr Bell with gratified interest. His was a strong face, she decided, without being particularly memorable. Afterwards she could recall little save an impression of pale eyes set in a pale well-shaven face. He was wearing the same colour and style of shirt as Oliver but his tie was different, and the badge that secured it a little more ornate.

'When I was young I always wanted to be a Girl Guide, but–'

'Excuse me–' He moved away to speak to someone else.

Disconcerted by his extreme brusqueness she surrendered her ticket, bought a programme and went to find her seat.

It was quite a large hall, a little bleak and chill, but the canvas chairs were tolerably comfortable and she could detect the glow of footlights behind the closed curtains up on the stage. After glancing through the programme in search of Oliver's name she began to look round at the other members of the audience; mostly mothers and fathers, brothers and sisters, she suspected, and turned in her seat in the hope of spotting Alastair's parents. It would be nice to see someone she knew, and she looked forward to the day when she had made a few more friends in the neighbourhood. Then the curtains jerked apart to disclose the neat figure of Amory Bell. He raised his hand for silence.

Welcoming them in a clear quiet voice, he went on to explain that the object of the concert was to show not merely the lighter side of being a Young Citizen, but also to give some idea of their aims and ideals. They all sounded very laudable. He then went on to admit with a deprecating little smile that the object of the concert was also to help raise funds for their proposed summer camp.

'We do not ask that the youth of this country be overindulged,' he said. 'We merely ask for a small percentage of the money lavished by successive governments on other, and I think less deserving, sections of our society. And while our pleas continue to be ignored we have no option but to ask for your help in providing some of the equipment still outstanding. We have already raised the money for four ex-army ridge tents and a field kitchen, and last year, if you remember, we were successful in our attempt to purchase a small second-hand pickup truck as a means of transport. But we still need such items as groundsheets, tarpaulins, large water containers and a portable fridge. There will be a collection at the end of the evening and you are asked to donate to it as generously as possible. The future of the world lies in the hands of the young and we must not let them down. Thank you.' He walked off to the sound of applause.

The lights were lowered and the concert began. There were some songs, a gymnastic display, and a sketch about a professor who had invented a magic shrinking machine. Into the tea chest painted with knobs and dials he put a large sheet, and after a few moments' whirring and rumbling drew out a small pocket handkerchief. The machine performed further miracles of a similar nature, and when the demonstration ended with a large plump boy climbing into the tea chest and then a small thin one in the form of Oliver springing gleefully out, Mrs Dansie laughed and applauded with unrestrained delight.

During the interval when cups of tea and tins of assorted biscuits were being passed along the rows of chairs, Oliver came to find her. He was brandishing a book of raffle tickets.

'It's for our camping fund.'

'What's the prize?'

'A book about wildlife.'

She bought six. 'You were very good in the sketch.'

'Yes. Know how it was done?'

'No idea.'

She was aware that the people on either side of her were listening and smiling. And Oliver, she could tell, was also aware. With sparkling eyes and big glistening teeth he explained, ostensibly to her, but in reality to the whole row. To the whole world, if it was listening.

'Easy. You see, I was in the machine all the time. I was crouching down in the bottom and when Martin got in – he's the big one – he fell on top of me and it was a job not to laugh.'

'It must have been a bit crowded in there,' Mrs Dansie was aware that she was playing to the gallery as much as he.

'Oh no, it was okay because we rehearsed it. We often do much harder things than that.'

'Yes, I'm sure. Are you in anything else?'

'No. But I've got to go back and be up there when we all march on and bow at the end.'

Aware that it would be demeaning to offer him a perch on her knees she made room for him on the corner of her chair. He accepted it, and she caught the salty tang of little boy sweat mingled with the smell of chewing gum and shoe polish.

The second half of the programme was devoted to more serious matters.

A first aid demonstration, a bicycle puncture mending race and an item about the preservation of the earth's resources.

The final piece also concerned conservation, but seemed to be set in a more light-hearted vein. The stage was strewn with a miscellany of torn paper, sweet wrappers, empty coke tins and broken cardboard boxes. Four boys with brooms began sweeping it all towards a row of dustbins while a dozen or so more boys, all of them older than Oliver, marched on stage to provide a chorus. Their clomping feet kept time with the chant.

What shall we do with the rubbish of life?
We'll tidy it up – we'll tidy it up!
What shall we do with the litter of life?
We'll – we'll tidy it up!–

Good for them, thought Mrs Dansie. Some of the streets are filthy these days.

A boy dressed as an old tramp with white hair sticking out from a battered top hat limped on, quavering insults and shaking a palsied fist at the sweepers. They brushed him out of the way.

What shall we do with the garbage of life?
We'll tidy it up – we'll tidy it up!–

The old tramp skipped nimbly out of the way and everyone laughed. The marching continued, the thumping feet shaking the stage.

What shall we do with industrial waste?
We'll tidy it up – we'll tidy it up!–

A Young Citizen with thick limbs and very

short hair picked up a cardboard container labelled Toxic Material and flung it into one of the dustbins. One or two people in the audience began to stamp their feet in unison. The rhythm of the chant was becoming mildly hypnotic.

Gradually the stage was cleared of paper and tins, all of it being hurled with increasing force into the waiting receptacles. The marching and chanting quickened, and the only non-conformist was the old tramp, who tottered wildly and senselessly, getting in the way and doing his best to impede progress. The young couple sitting to the right of Mrs Dansie were laughing so heartily that she wondered if they were his parents.

She glanced at Oliver. He was crouching forward on his bit of the seat with his hands pressed tightly between his knees and his tongue moving to and fro in rhythm with the chanting and stamping. In every child there's a little pack animal, she thought. Thank God this isn't the Hitler Youth Movement.

'It's good, isn't it?' she whispered. He nodded without removing his gaze from the stage.

What shall we do with the sewage and sludge?
We'll tidy it up – we'll tidy it up!

The tramp capered more preposterously than ever, reeling, staggering, and uttering quavering cries almost drowned by the steadily increasing din. Everyone in the audience was clapping and stamping, and then came the inevitable moment:

What shall we do with the dirt and dregs?
We'll tidy it up – WE'LL TIDY IT UP!

And the sweepers flung down their brooms, seized the tramp and bore him kicking and struggling to the last dustbin. His top hat rolled off and there was a fleeting glimpse of chaotic cotton wool hair before he was bundled unceremoniously inside, shoved deep down, and then the lid slammed back in place. The curtains closed on a stage now swept bare as a bone and on a row of Young Citizens beaming hotly under the lights, while the agile figure of the tramp sprang out of the dustbin to redoubled applause from the audience. Mrs Dansie applauded too, happy to be a part of the family community.

She and Oliver walked home along the quiet road where the chestnut trees were already casting a summer shadow.

'I thought the boy who played the tramp was very good.'

'He's my friend.'

'What's his name?'

'Alastair. You've met him.'

'So I have. He came up to my flat with his parents, didn't he?'

'He's got to have his ears syringed on Monday.'

'Oh, poor Alastair.'

They walked on in silence, Oliver's head a glimmering blob reaching between her elbow and her shoulder. She paused by a garden wall, inhaling the scent from a spray of overhanging flowers. He waited politely.

'What's that flower called?'

'When I was young we used to call it mock orange, but now it's known as philadelphus.'

'Why?'

'I don't know, unless it's a sign that we're getting more formal with plants as we get more informal with people. Calling it mock orange is like calling me Granny when my real name is Celia Dansie.'

'Can flowers ever be grandmothers?'

'Oh, yes. But I don't suppose they're ever conscious of the fact that they are.'

'Do you like it, being a grandmother?'

'Yes, I do,' she said. 'I like it very much.'

The warm night seemed to have extinguished the smell of petrol fumes and hot macadam roads so that the big sprawling gardens could have their turn. Azaleas, paeonies, early philadelphus, and the cool damp smell of ferns growing in brickwork. Dark cats slipped in and out of the shadows.

'I do agree with the idea of tidying things up,' Mrs Dansie remarked. 'It's all very well to invent all these marvellous things but we mustn't let them get the upper hand.'

'Mr Bell says that when things are old and worn out we've got to get rid of them. It's no use being sentimental.'

'We'll tidy them up, we'll tidy them up…'

'And he says it ought to be the same with people.'

'Oh. Well yes, I suppose it ought, in theory.'

'I could have been the tramp just as good as Alastair was.'

'I'm sure you could. Perhaps next time it'll be your turn.'

They reached their own dark gateway and walked up the drive, their footsteps muffled by small weeds.

'Do you think Mummy and Daddy are back from their meeting yet?'

'There aren't many lights on.'

'But the baby-sitter will still be there, won't she?'

'Yes. Her name's Penny and she's stupid.'

Together they peered towards the big house, its Victorian roofline standing harsh against the reddish outer London skyline.

'Let's go and see if their car's back.'

It wasn't.

'Oliver, are you feeling peckish?'

'Yes.'

'Come on, then.'

Upstairs in her kitchen they made two cups of milky coffee and a pile of hot buttered toast.

71

'If you look in that cupboard you'll find some honey. Or would you rather have jam?'

'What sort is it?'

'Strawberry, I think.'

He settled for some of both, and she produced another knife so that he could apply the final covering after she had spread the butter.

'At home they'd have made me wash my hands first.'

'And so would I,' Mrs Dansie said heartily, 'if only I'd remembered.'

They loaded the tray and took it through to the main room.

'The week they said Alastair could be the tramp was the week I was away,' Oliver said.

'I thought you were very good in the shrinking machine sketch.'

'Yes, but I didn't have any words.'

'Neither did the tramp. He just made silly little noises.'

'That's all old people ever do.'

'Is it?' She looked at him in surprise.

'Oh yes. They just hop about in everybody's way and make little quavery noises that don't make sense.'

She began to laugh. 'When I start to do that will you please tell me?'

It was his turn to look surprised. With his mouth full of toast he sat considering her, summing her up as if he had never really seen her before.

'How old are you?'

'I'll be sixty at the beginning of September.'

'It does sound very old,' he admitted. 'But you don't really seem it.'

'Don't you like old people?'

'I don't know.' He looked evasive. 'They're all right.'

She finished her coffee and pushed the cup and saucer away. 'Tell me some more riddles.'

'Okay.' The evasive look disappeared. 'What's the difference between a plane and a tree?'

'I don't know.'

'One leaves its shed and the other sheds its leaves.'

'That's a good one. Now – what lies at the bottom of the sea and shivers?'

'Dunno.'

'A nervous wreck.'

'Huh.' But he began to laugh because she was laughing and the sound they made prevented them from hearing the voices and footsteps on the stairs.

'Well, well,' Willow said, a dramatic figure in the doorway. 'What are you two naughty people up to?'

She came into the room followed by Seth.

'When we got back we discovered that we were rather hungry,' Mrs Dansie explained. It occurred to her that she might appear a little ingenuous sitting on the floor with her shoes kicked off. Unobtrusively she wiped the honey from her fingers.

'We've had some coffee as well,' Oliver said.

'Have you really?' Seth's beard parted to reveal his smile. 'My gosh, Mummy, I don't know whether it's a good thing to leave these two alone together.'

'I know. I'm beginning to think they get up to all sorts of mischief as soon as our backs are turned.'

The Mitchells surveyed Mrs Dansie and Oliver with mock alarm, their eyes very big and their mouths pursed very small. Oliver giggled, and then caught his breath. He coughed toast crumbs over the carpet. And Mrs Dansie looked up at his parents and thought: They've got that warm, surreptitious look of two people who have just been to bed together. But I thought they'd gone to a meeting about ethnic races...

'How did the concert go?' With his arm round Willow, Seth led her over to the sofa. They both sat down.

'It was very, very good,' Mrs Dansie said. 'Can I make you both some coffee?'

They declined, saying that it was long past Oliver's bedtime and that the sitter-in was waiting to go home.

'When I was in the washing machine Martin jumped in on top of me and we couldn't stop laughing–'

'Oliver made a marvellous job of his part–'

'And I had to go up on stage at the end and bow with all the others–'

'You really would have been very proud of him,' Mrs Dansie said, feeling ingenuous again.

'But Alastair got the best part. They made him the tramp, but I could have done it much better.'

Oliver gave a demonstration, reeling and tottering with trembling limbs and his eyes rolled up. He trod in his cup and saucer and the teaspoon flew up and hit him on the chin.

'Ow-ow-ow!' He hopped in simulated agony, clutching his lower jaw. He fell, and lay writhing, while Mrs Dansie bubbled with laughter.

'We must take our wild animal home.' Seth stood up, then reached down for Willow's hand. They stood together with their arms linked, and the warm surreptitious look was even more marked.

'Listen, Oliver,' Willow said, 'we want your opinion – and Granny's – about something rather special. What would you say to the idea of us making a home for a little refugee from Uganda?'

'Where?' Oliver stopped writhing and stood up. 'In this house?'

'Over in our house, yes.'

'Why?'

'Because Daddy and I have been to a film which showed us how absolutely dreadful their living conditions are. None of them have enough to eat, some of them are even starving, and they haven't even got clean water to drink like we have. They've got nothing, Oliver, and yet they're all just ordinary nice children like you and Humphrey and–'

'Would it be a boy or a girl?'

'If we could afford it,' Seth said, 'Mummy and I thought it would be rather fun to have one of each. There'd be a lot of details to fix up, of course–'

'Not that Daddy and I think of children as *details*, exactly.' Willow released herself from Seth and drew Oliver close. She straightened his Young Citizen's tie. 'To us, children are very important people – every single living person is very important – and when we find out about some poor people who haven't got one hundredth of all the lovely things that we've got, well naturally, we want to share some of them. After all, it's only fair, isn't it?'

Oliver stood thinking, while Willow's hand left his tie and began to stroke his rumpled bob of hair.

'Will it have to be in my bedroom?'

'No, not necessarily. There's the little room where we do the ironing, for instance–'

'And will Granny have to be its Granny too?'

Willow and Seth turned their loving smiles upon Mrs Dansie, who braced herself a little.

'I'm willing to share my happiness with anyone who needs it,' she said, and tried to catch Oliver's eye so that she might send him a wink of reassurance. But he remained staring down at the toes of his shoes.

'Come on, old son,' Seth ruffled the bob of hair that Willow had just finished stroking down flat. 'Time you and Granny were both tucked up asleep.'

'Goodnight, my dears.' Mrs Dansie bent to pick up the cups and saucers. She retrieved the teaspoon from where it had landed. 'Goodnight, Oliver, and thank you for inviting me to the concert.'

She went to bed soon afterwards, and towards dawn was wrenched from sleep by what seemed less like a dream than a sudden violent realisation. Among all the people who had packed the hall at the concert she had been the only elderly member; the only one, apart from Alastair's ludicrously capering tramp, to have white hair.

She sat up, staring into the darkness and trying to calm herself by remembering the innocent jollity of the evening, but all impression of innocence and jollity had fled. In its place had appeared an undercurrent of menace, something baleful and sinister, and with a shock she realised that it had its origins in the cold pale eyes of Mr Bell during that brief moment when he looked at her.

Amory Bell's grandmother had been a large woman with heavy dewlaps and feet that bulged over her shoes. She was his father's mother, and had lived alone in the house in Ilford for some ten years before Amory joined her. Her husband had died of a strangulated hernia, which she always referred to as a perforated appendix because it sounded more respectable.

The three-bedroomed terrace house appeared to Amory to be very large after the cramped theatrical digs he had been used to, and he stood wriggling slightly in the middle of what seemed like a limitless expanse of glittering linoleum as they tried to explain once more that he was going to live with his Gran like a big boy while Mum and Dad worked hard to earn pennies to keep him.

'You're going to school on Monday and when you come home Gran'll have something extra nice for your tea, and then you'll be able to tell her all about how you got on, won't you?' his father said.

But his mother dispersed any grains of confidence by clutching at him tearfully and saying 'It won't be for long, ducky. Just stay here a little while and then we'll all be together again just like we used to be.'

Chilled and confused, his torment was

intensified by an increasing need to go to the lavatory, but he didn't know where it was and didn't like to ask.

'You and Gran'll get on fine together.' His father tried to pull his mother's arms away. 'You'll be a couple of real close pals in no time.'

Amory began to cry, tears pouring down his cheeks like rain-drops while he tried unavailingly to explain at least some of the thousand reasons why they shouldn't go away and leave him. But the words wouldn't come, and anyway they wouldn't listen, and the tears dripped down onto the linoleum and he had to stand with his legs crossed because he wanted to go to the lavatory so much.

They left the house very hurriedly, his grandmother bundling them out of the door while she kept saying 'Stop hanging about – get it over with quick–' and then the door banged and she came back into the room and stood looking down at him in the way that a bloodhound might look down at a beetle.

'Well, my lad,' she said finally. 'What have you got to say for yourself?'

'I want to wee,' he said. But it was too late, and the stream of water splashed onto the floor and obliterated all the sad little circles of his tears.

She wasn't a bad woman, any more than Amory was a difficult child, but they never grew to like one another. To begin with he cried so much, wanting his mother in the helpless inarticulate fashion of some small unweaned animal, yet on the occasion that his grandmother attempted to kiss him he turned his face away, repelled by the stubble on her dewlaps.

Perhaps it would have eased the intolerable sense of loss if she had encouraged him to talk about the old life spent between dressing-rooms and theatrical digs, but this she was not prepared to do, firstly because of a genuine fear of increasing his misery and secondly because of her own very strong antipathy towards people who pranced about on the stage and showed themselves off. She had never forgiven her son for his choice of occupation, or for his choice of a wife.

Rooted in Chapel and convinced of the twin evils of alcohol and the flesh, it seemed only right that if she was being asked to bring up the child she should be free to do so in the manner she considered correct. So music hall songs were replaced by Sankey and Moody and she made a big thing of not allowing him to put his hands in his trouser pockets unless it was to remove or replace his handkerchief. She kept him very clean and well-fed but she never talked to him. And she certainly never laughed. She never thought that anything was either funny or beautiful, it was either right or not right, and when she discovered the pathetic remains of his mother's old swansdown powderpuff hidden inside his pillowcase she could only see it as something strangely lewd and lascivious. She washed her hands after throwing it away.

The first time his parents came to see him he was almost ill with excitement; love, and a frantic desire to secure their undivided attention made him behave badly. He jumped up and down on the couch with his shoes on, swaggered about with hands thrust defiantly in his trouser pockets and cried with rage at being made to eat up his crusts at teatime.

He was sent to bed, and when his mother came up to say goodbye the old familiar smell of make-up and cheap scent drove him insane with the hunger to be close to her again. Sitting up in a wild pinging of bed-springs he plunged his hands down the neck of her blouse while he covered her face with feverish kisses. She kissed him back with equal warmth, then suddenly pushed him away.

'Here,' she said, 'what's your Gran been teaching you? You're a bit too young for that sort of thing.'

But she gave him a sixpence wrapped up in a scrap of tissue paper and promised to bring him some comics next time they came. She made him promise to be a good boy, and when she went out of the door he knew that she didn't look back because she was crying as hard as he was.

They came again when they were playing a club in Leytonstone, but they forgot to bring the comics.

He was quite bright at school, but quickly grew to dislike the opprobrium earned by being keen on lessons. His classmates jeered, and roughed him up a couple of times; but when, in an attempt to win their approval, he deliberately came bottom in arithmetic his teacher wrote a nasty little note to his Gran and he was allowed no cake or pudding for two weeks. Furthermore she refused to look at him, even when issuing the complaints and commands that were her only form of communication with him.

By the time he was ten he knew that he would never live with his parents any more. They still came to see him, but separately, and then his father stopped coming altogether. His Gran remained tight-lipped, while his mother, when he asked her, said that Daddy was working a long way away but sent his love. One day she brought a strange man with her; he was wearing a drape suit and thick crêpe-soled shoes but Gran made him wait outside in the street while his mother came in and tried to make bright conversation in a shrill, shaky little voice. And he couldn't help counting all the times she glanced out of the front room window to make sure that the man was still there.

Then she stopped coming too, but by now it didn't matter because he didn't need her any more. He didn't need anyone very much, and with some of the money he earned doing a newspaper round he bought himself a small secondhand tent and took himself off for weekends in Epping Forest. A quiet, pale, unobtrusive boy, he became absorbed by the idea of self-sufficiency, and lying alone in the dark after a good meal cooked on the primus stove he would come close to a state of exaltation at the sound of wind and rain and scuttering leaves outside the simple neatness of his own private sanctuary. The knowledge that he could take care of himself was of far greater value than that of any friendship. As for girls, they didn't exist.

It seemed for a while as if this chill aloofness was the precise quality his Gran had striven to induce in him during all these years; she nagged less, criticised seldom, and it was not until his fifteenth birthday that he became aware that some of the other changes taking place in her had nothing to do with his behaviour. The small birthday cake she had made suddenly dropped from her hands and smashed on the floor while she stood looking at it with a kind of tired wonderment. He then noticed how slowly she moved, shuffling with bent head and bowed shoulders and sometimes taking as long as five minutes to climb the stairs. He had never realised how much her hands shook, and when she seemed to have grown too lethargic even to wipe away the small bead of saliva from the corner of her mouth it was fairly obvious that she refrained from nagging because she could no longer be bothered to do so. He knew that people became doddery with old age, but the thoughtful streak in him warned that this might be something different. He told her that she should go to the doctor for a tonic. She refused, so on the way home from school he called at the surgery and asked for a visit.

The doctor came, and then took Amory into the front room and closed the door. He began by asking what other members of the family could be called on to give assistance, and was visibly startled when Amory said What do we want assistance for?

'Your grandma is very ill with something that can't be cured very easily,' the doctor said. 'It's called Parkinson's disease.'

And the Parkinson's disease changed a lot of things for Amory.

Instead of going on to Walthamstow Technical College he left school and got a job in a radio repair shop round the corner so that he could go home at dinnertime to boil the potatoes and warm the stew. He looked after his Gran with extraordinary competence, doing a little more for her each week, but it never occurred to him to talk to her. The long years of taciturnity had bitten deeply into his character, but with his newly acquired electrical knowledge he rigged up a buzzer which she could jab with her elbow if she wanted anything. She seldom used it.

The house grew even quieter, until there was only the tick of the clock and the dim rumble of traffic at the end of the road. Sometimes it seemed as if there was a particular density in the silence surrounding the motionless figure in the kitchen armchair. It lay about her in heavy folds; warm, stale and claustrophobic. In the evenings he would sit opposite her, trying to read but finding his attention constantly drawn to the quivering dewlaps and the eyes that stared at him with such a terrible blank intensity.

'All right? Want anything?'

Sometimes with a superhuman effort she would give her head a jerk but there was no means of discovering what significance, if any, lay in the movement.

The district nurse called every day, and once when she met Amory coming home from the shop she asked if he ever went out in the evenings. Her homely face expressed concern when he said no, and she started talking about the importance of having an outside hobby. Did he like sport?

No, not particularly, he told her, but something impelled him to add that he used to like going camping all on his own in

Epping Forest. She listened as he described the tent to her, and the way in which it could be folded and transported by bicycle and how easy it was to look after yourself with the minimum of equipment once you got the hang of it.

'It sounds a grand way of getting away from it all,' she said. 'I think I'll come with you.'

To begin with he thought she meant it, and acute apprehension made him careful to avoid her at all costs, then as the days went by and nothing further developed he realised that she must have been joking. In any case she was only too aware of the burden that tied him to the house.

But the mere mention of camping brought back the memories of two years ago when he used to set off after tea on Fridays, weaving in and out of the irritable commuter rush until it was all left behind and there was nothing but the quiet purr of his tyres and the rustle of leaves overhead. Now that those weekends were gone for ever he was convinced that he had not appreciated them sufficiently; that he should have wrung even more enjoyment from each hour spent in keeping house for himself in the lonely beauty of Epping Forest.

Spooning tinned chicken soup between his Gran's sagging, trembling lips he thought for the first time how easy it would be to end her misery and his by pressing a cushion over her face.

During the week following the Young Citizens' concert Oliver's conviction that he could have played the part of the old tramp better than Alastair refused to fade. Instead, it seemed to grow more persistent, nagging away like a splinter in the finger until its presence began to show signs of poisoning the very friendship itself.

He thought about Alastair a lot, and came to the conclusion that he was a bighead and a nit, and once or twice when he was up in his grandmother's flat he wished that she would mention Alastair's name so that he might be persuaded to divulge the truth about him. But she didn't mention it, and because Oliver didn't wish to demean himself by telling tales, he didn't mention it either. But he no longer sought Alastair's company on the walk home from school or from Young Citizens', preferring to amble along on his own while he pictured new items in new concerts in which Oliver Mitchell played the leading role. For the first time he began to experience the heady pleasure of inventing situations of which he was hero, and the applause that sang in his ears was no less gratifying because it was imaginary. He discovered that he needed applause; from his teachers, from his family, but most of all, for some reason, from Mr Bell.

So it was all the more disagreeable when Alastair waylaid him by his gateway one afternoon and said without preamble: 'Mr Bell's fed up with you.'

Startled out of a sweet dream involving coming top in insect recognition, Oliver stared at him.

'Why?'

'Because you brought your grandmother to the concert.'

'My mother and father couldn't go.'

'That's no excuse for taking your grandmother.'

'Why shouldn't I have?'

Alastair's expression became sly. Bighead and nit he might be, there was a laconic self-possession about him that Oliver had never noticed before. It also made him realise that Alastair was not only fatter, but was also a little bit taller.

'Why shouldn't I have?' For some reason it was easier to stand there and repeat the question rather than walk away.

'Because nobody else did. Nobody else's grandmother *or* grandfather was there, and there's a special reason why they weren't.'

'Well, *why?*'

'It's a secret.'

'And you're a fat nit. You're stupid and thick and you've got bunged up ears.'

'Well, I haven't see? They squirted a lot of

hot water in and all sorts of poison stuff came out.'

'It was only wax.'

'No it wasn't, it was something special.'

'Huh.'

They stood staring at one another with hard eyes and set mouths, mutual dislike developing like some kind of fungoid growth between them. At last Oliver dug his hands deep in his pockets and began to walk stiffly away.

'Goodnight, ratface.'

'Same to you, elephant bum.'

'And you can say Big Goodnight to your stupid old grandmother from me.'

Oliver halted. His grandmother was very nearly old but she wasn't stupid, and he began retracing his steps with the idea of telling Alastair so; of even punching him, if he was able to catch him unawares. But Alastair was now sitting on the gate while it swung to and fro, and instead of vindicating his grandmother Oliver looked up at him with a strange yearning from which all anger had melted.

'If you tell me what Big Goodnight means, I promise I won't let on to anyone you told me.'

Alastair seemed to soften too. He contemplated Oliver in silence for a moment, then patted the top rail of the gate where he was sitting. Oliver scrambled up and they sat hunched close together, their knees and shoulders touching.

'Don't you really know?'

'Wouldn't ask if I did.'

'Cross your heart and hope to die if you tell?'

Oliver crossed and hoped.

'Well, it means,' Alastair said in a guttural whisper, 'killing people. Killing them when they get old and no good to anybody, because Mr Bell says that our planet's getting overcrowded and so it's only fair.'

'But killing people's wrong.' Oliver's mouth had become very dry.

'Not if it's legal, it isn't. If they pass a law saying you can, then it's all right.'

'But there isn't–'

'Nigel Schofield's brother told him there's going to be before long, and then it won't need to be secret any more.'

A sense of horrified fascination gripped Oliver. It seemed to glue him to the top rail of Alastair's gate so that although part of him wanted to run home and hear no more, he lacked the ability to move. He swallowed hard.

'I know they kill a lot of people on telly, but it's only made up,' he ventured finally.

'This is real.'

'No, it's not.' He didn't sound convinced, even to his own ears. 'It's a lot of lies.'

'Suit yourself,' Alastair said. 'But if you

tell, they'll kill you too.'

They sat in silence watching a large blue Peugeot creep down the road, hesitate, then turn in at a gateway. Oliver felt drained, almost ill with the effort of trying not to believe what Alastair had just told him.

'How do they kill them?'

'Oh, I don't think it hurts.' Alastair was splendidly offhand. 'They just give them an injection or make them drink something that puts them to sleep. And Mr Bell told Nigel's brother that although the idea isn't legal yet, he thinks that people can be trained to get used to the idea of killing themselves sort of quietly when they get to sixty years old, and nobody'll mind because they'll all be used to it, see? And once they're all used to it, they'll make it legal.'

'But supposing they don't want to kill themselves?'

'Then somebody'll have to do it for them, instead.'

'Who?'

'Dunno. Probably their sons or their daughters, or maybe the doctor.'

'Perhaps they could escape,' Oliver said hopefully.

'You just don't get it, do you?' Alastair's voice sounded tired and elderly. 'It won't be anything to do with whether they want to die or not, they'll just die because they've been brought up to the idea of dying when

91

they get to sixty. After all, everybody's got to die sometime, haven't they?'

'Yes, but not on a certain day. And not just because the Queen or somebody tells you you've got to.'

'Don't see it makes much difference.' Alastair fumbled in the pocket that was on the far side of Oliver and drew out a raspberry-coloured boiled sweet. Meditatively he began to pluck the fluff off it. 'Anyway, that's what Big Goodnight means, and if you tell anyone else about it you won't get to ten, let alone sixty.'

'Would they *really* kill me?'

'You bet they would. They'd give the order straight away.'

'But who's *they?*' Oliver asked worriedly. He watched Alastair remove the last fragment of fluff from his sweet before putting it in his mouth. He felt the water gathering round his own tongue in envy.

'The Organisation,' Alastair said. 'They wear black masks and have death-ray guns and they can get into places even when the doors and windows are locked…'

But he had gone too far, and his words merely succeeded in bringing a profound sense of relief to Oliver. Spacemen, monsters and death-rays were something he could cope with; they all belonged to the happy world of make-believe and made it possible to relegate the explanation of Big Goodnight to the same mental toy cupboard. It was something seen on TV, something dreamed up deliciously while lying safely in bed at night.

'They don't really kill old people,' Oliver said with new confidence. 'They just sort of paralyse them for the time being and then fly them out to another planet.'

'Well, you'll soon find out, won't you?' Alastair said amiably, and gazed ahead of him while the boiled sweet rattled slowly and comfortably round his teeth. The road was very quiet, and they heard the slam of car doors and the scrunch of feet on gravel. Voices called hullo to the people who had arrived in the blue Peugeot.

'My auntie's coming home from America next week,' Alastair said at length. 'And one day she's going to take me back there for a holiday.'

'How old is she?'

'Dunno. Why?'

Oliver sat without answering, trying to get used to the sudden new importance of people's ages; the awful fascination, already gripping him, of working out how much longer they'd got, just supposing that Big Goodnight was real. He wondered how much longer Mr Bell had got, then drew reassurance from the thought that as one of the senior exponents of the scheme he might well be disqualified from taking part. He very much hoped so.

'She's going to show me Disneyland and the Empire State Building.'

'Huh,' Oliver said absently. He himself had fifty-one and a half years to go, an expanse of time so great that it was virtually meaningless.

'I'll be the only one at school *and* at Young Citizens that's been to America, and Mr Bell says I've got to keep a diary about everything I see and let him read it out to everybody when I get back.'

Forgetting about people's ages, Oliver felt stirrings of the old resentful jealousy. Surely it was enough to have been the tramp in the concert without going to America as well? As for Mr Bell asking him to keep a diary – everyone knew that Alastair Grant was a big thick nit who couldn't even spell words like helicopter.

'Well, we're going to adopt some Ugandans.'

'What for?'

'Because – well, because we all owe them something.'

'You don't believe I'm going to America, do you?' Alastair stopped rattling his sweet and started to crunch it belligerently.

'No.'

'You don't believe about my auntie either, do you?'

'No.'

'Well, it just shows you're stupid. She's nice, and she knows the President and I'm going to stay with her. My parents both say!'

Suddenly irritated beyond endurance, Oliver jumped down from the gate and began to walk towards his own home. He could feel Alastair's gaze making a hole in his back, but it didn't matter because all he wanted was to go away and think about things in peace.

Even so, he stopped when Alastair called his name. Stopped, and turned round, but didn't retrace his steps. They were about fifteen feet apart, Alastair still crouched on the top of the gate with his elbows on his knees while Oliver stood motionless.

'And what I told you about the other thing is real, too. If you don't believe me, wait and see.'

He certainly looked as if he was telling the truth; he wasn't laughing, or in a temper, he just looked very serious. Oliver's confidence began to waver. The dry feeling came back into his mouth again.

'Goodnight, weasel head.' The words didn't come out very clearly, but they were better than nothing.

He turned and began to walk towards his own gateway, but the moment he was through it he started to run with his head down and his fists bunched close to his armpits. Like an animal making for the sanctuary of its bolt hole he made for the granny flat, then realised with a sense of shock exactly what Alastair had meant when he said that he would soon find out whether or not it was true about Big Goodnight.

He remembered having told him that his grandmother was going to celebrate her sixtieth birthday a few days after they got back from camp; he also remembered boasting of the fact that she had already invited him to the party.

Willow was sitting cross-legged on the kitchen floor with her arms outstretched at either side and her fingertips lightly touching the sisal matting. Her head was raised, her impressive nose pointing towards the window.

It was a big kitchen, picturesque in its untidiness, with many surfaces covered in check gingham and a great many ivies and herbs and busy lizzies scrambling over French cooking utensils and wholefood cookery books. Humphrey, in stretch tights and a jumper, was sitting under the antique pine table, rocking backwards and forwards and sucking his thumb.

His world was now an oscillating jumble of bright objects, seemingly desirable but proving on closer inspection to be of dubious value. So many of them had hard surfaces, sharp edges and a disagreeable taste. His mother's world, on the other hand, was a kind of silver blue void through which she floated, serene as a lotus petal, calm as a basking trout. Detached from all the minor irritations of life, she was aware only of harmony, of an abstract sense of well-being. She was weightless, formless, a breath of quiet summer air imbued with a strange and infinite benevolence.

The kitchen door opened and Mrs Dansie appeared.

'Oh – am I interrupting something?'

'No, not at all. Come in Granny.'

Slowly and without any sign of self-consciousness Willow abandoned her Yoga position and stood up. It was a source of quiet envy in Mrs Dansie that she could stand up without using her hands as a means of leverage.

'I was just going shopping,' Mrs Dansie said, 'and wondered if you wanted anything. I was also wondering how you've been getting on with the adoption of your little Ugandans. I haven't heard any more since the night you first broke the news.' Wearing a dark linen suit and sandals she looked alert and businesslike.

'No thank you to the first question,' Willow said, and going over to the pine dresser took down two glass tumblers. 'As to the second, well obviously it's going to take a little time to wade through all the tiresome formalities. First we've got to get permission to get them out of Uganda, and having achieved that there's a mass more paperwork to be gone through before they can enter this country. Crazy, when you think of it.'

'But you're still keen?' Seeing Humphrey under the table Mrs Dansie bent down and chirruped to him.

'Of course we're still keen. After all, it's a matter of saving human life, isn't it?'

'Yes. It's also a very long and serious commitment.'

'So are Oliver and Humphrey.'

Willow took a jug from the fridge and began to pour its contents into the two tumblers. 'Have some juice.'

Mrs Dansie thanked her, and sipped a little gingerly. Most liquids drunk in her daughter's household were of an undefinable nature and referred to as juice. This one was thin, brown and rather cloudy, and like all the others, packed with health-giving properties.

'Do sit down, Granny,' Willow said, and Mrs Dansie did so, conscious that this was only the third time she had ventured uninvited into her daughter's domain.

Willow perched herself on the edge of the table and regarded her with affectionate concern. 'You haven't got any sort of prejudice against the black races, have you?'

'Good heavens, no,' Mrs Dansie said quickly and very sincerely. 'None whatever. I'd want you to feel just as certain of yourselves if you were adopting a child from the next road.'

'But naturally we're certain. After all, it shouldn't take much deliberation before opening your family circle to someone dreadfully in need, should it? It should be a natural, spontaneous gesture and nothing more.'

'Yes, ideally it should. But darling, before you take on such a serious responsibility you must consider it from all angles. For instance, supposing...'

'Yes?'

Mrs Dansie sighed and took another sip of brown juice. With Willow looking at her so kindly and so healthily it was difficult to ask what would happen if either she or Seth died. Or the practice failed, or if nuclear war broke out.

'I hope Oliver won't feel usurped,' she mumbled finally.

'Oh, I rather doubt it, for the simple reason that he's being brought up to care about other people. Seth and I, you may have noticed, care a lot about other people's welfare–' For a moment Willow subjected her mother to a meaningful stare, from which her mother instinctively retreated.

'Yes dear, I know – I have every reason to–'

'Oh come off it, I'm not referring to you. All I'm trying to say is that wanting to share what we have with other people comes naturally to us. And I'm not just talking about Seth and me. All our friends feel the same way; we all feel this rather special sense of responsibility towards the basic components of life, and I can't help thinking that Oliver is developing quite well in that direction, considering that he's still only a little boy–'

'He's absolutely sweet to me, always,' Mrs Dansie said, accepting her role as a basic component, 'and that brings me to another point. I haven't seen much of him for the past few days. He generally pops up to see me after school, but–'

'I think he's been playing with Alastair... But you see, caring for people should be as natural as breathing–'

'Should be–'

'And it seems as if the whole world is waking up to that fact at last. I mean, at last the ideas of ordinary decent people are beginning to predominate. Take the Young Citizens while we're on the subject of Oliver. They're not a bit Queen and country and salute the flag like the Boy Scouts were – or are. I believe there are still some about. No, that conception is completely outmoded, for which I, for one, profoundly thank God–'

'I must say Mr Bell struck me as a bit, well – formidable...'

'He's what they call their Citizen Leader, isn't he? Yes, obviously, his influence is very strong, which is marvellous when you know that he's helping to teach them all the right ideas as well. So you see, with all the right ideas coming from us *and* the Young Citizens *and* the present day teaching in schools, they can't help but cohere in our children's minds, can they?'

Willow suddenly stretched out her hand and touched Mrs Dansie's white hair with an affectionate little gesture. 'So you mustn't *worry* about things, Granny. There aren't nearly as many problems as some older people think, and even then, none of the problems are insoluble.'

Because I was young I had no terrors during the London blitz, thought Mrs Dansie and stood up. She and her daughter smiled at one another fondly, yet with a certain emptiness. Mrs Dansie said that she must be going to the shops before they closed for lunch and Willow said that she had to deliver some drawings to the planning department in Kingston.

'What about Humphrey?'

'I'm taking him with me.'

'Oh yes,' said Mrs Dansie. 'Of course.'

She waited while Humphrey was hauled from under the table, and his tightly padded bottom sniffed at.

'No problems?'

'No problems at all,' Willow said, and settled him in the crook of her beautiful thin arm.

So they parted, Mrs Dansie filled with love, some slight misgiving, and the ignominious wish that she might no longer be addressed as Granny as if it were her Christian name.

Most of all she wished that Oliver would call to see her later on after school.

Amory Bell didn't murder his grandmother. She died slowly and without interference, sinking a little deeper each day into the impenetrable depths that the district nurse termed her happy release.

Three days before the end they wanted to move her to hospital, suddenly aware that the strain was unsuitable for a boy of Amory's age, but he showed surprising resistance to the idea. They marvelled to one another that such an outwardly phlegmatic youth should show such devotion. Dog-like, they called it, never realising that the horror of her moribund old carcass was only surpassed by the horror of being all alone in the house without her. Solitude appealed to him, especially the quiet clean solitude of Epping Forest, but the thought of the house without her physical presence appalled him. Believing neither in a ghost that would haunt him nor a God that would comfort him, he sensed nevertheless that the place would never be free of her. Finally released from the big bed with its oak beading and art silk counterpane, there would be no knowing where she might lurk;

watching, spying, and breathing heavy censoriousness from the shadows.

She died in the afternoon at about four o'clock, and his first intimation was when he arrived home from work and the district nurse said I'm afraid she's gone, dear. Don't go in just yet.

So he hung about downstairs, making a cup of tea but forgetting to drink it, while the nurse passed to and fro with bowls of clean water and big packs of cellulose wadding.

'You've been a wonderful boy,' she kept saying. 'I've never known a boy as wonderful as you.'

When it came to making the funeral arrangements they asked him where his parents were, and he said that they were both dead; which was only half a lie because he had not seen either of them for so long, it was possible that they might be. Never having been to a funeral before he was not discomforted by the lack of mourners; on the contrary, he was surprised that the wife of his employer should turn up, and merely resigned to the rambling presence of an old woman from five doors away who wore a balaclava helmet and believe that we were all descended from eels. She always turned up at everything.

But directly the funeral was over they forgot all about him, and had no idea of the torment he endured. It was even worse than he had feared, and for several months he refused to set foot inside the house until his accustomed bedtime was well past and he was almost stupid with fatigue. He worked for long hours repairing radios, toasters and electric irons, then after a snack in a coffee bar spent the remainder of the evening in the public library; he was a voracious reader who absorbed and retained everything he read, but the time always came when at last he had to insert his key in the lock and step inside the silent lino-floored house that still smelt of drugs and dying and the bowls of pink disinfectant the nurse had used. He would force himself to stare at her empty bed; at the washstand swept clear now of pill bottles and paper tissues, and wonder where she was. He didn't believe in anything – in anything at all – yet it was hard not to suspect that some intangible essence of her still lingered in the corners or clung batlike to the folds in the curtains.

It was a knock on the door one Saturday evening that saved him. A little boy thin as a sparrow shook a collecting tin at him and asked him to buy a flag for the Young Citizens.

'What's the Young Citizens?' Amory held the door close, as if afraid the boy might fly inside and perch on something.

'It's our club where we go every week. It's like the Cubs only better and we go camping in Epping Forest and we're getting up a concert next week and if you buy a ticket you can come.'

He bought one. Somewhat against his better judgement he went to the concert, and the Citizen Leader, a jovial man in horn-rimmed glasses, saw him standing alone and said: 'You're not one of the parents, are you?'

'No.'

'Friend of one of the boys?'

'No. Not really.'

'I see. Just a sort of friend in general.' He smiled briskly at Amory while his experienced eyes took in the neat nondescript clothes, the anonymous haircut and the pale reticent features. 'In that case, why don't you come round one evening and give us a hand? We're always on the lookout for chaps who'd be interested to help promote our ideas – broadly speaking we're an ecological group believing in keeping a tighter grip on technology, and all that – ever go camping, by the way?'

And the rest was easy. It seemed as if Amory Bell and the League of Young Citizens had been waiting for one another since time began.

Unused to, and by now unneedful of any close human affection, he found the relationships that flourished there exactly to his taste; friendly but impersonal, helpful yet breezily aloof. And once accustomed to the novel idea that other people might wish to seek him out, it was surprising what a lot he had to give. He himself was quite surprised by the wide range of skills and practical knowledge he had automatically acquired during the long period of keeping house and assuming responsibility for an invalid, and the surprise was rendered even more agreeable by the fact that so much of it could be put to excellent use in this new milieu. The public library saw him no more, unless it was to check something in the reference section.

And at the same time, with a mind become suddenly ravenous for an acceptable ideology he welcomed the new creed of environmental responsibility, of showing respect and concern towards all facets of life rather than that of the human race alone. To begin with it put everything into perspective for him, and even more than that, its healthy commonsense banished the chill chapel-laden gloom of his grandmother's house. As if he were at last waking up he realised that he needn't live there any more if he didn't want to. That as her sole heir he was legally entitled to sell it and buy another place somewhere else. And strangest of all, with the dawning of realisation came peace and the immediate cessation of all the nameless lurking horrors he had suffered in the months since her death.

He packed up all her personal effects, clothes, hairbrushes, handbags and pictures of the Good Shepherd, and they fetched seventeen pounds at the Young Citizens' Christmas bazaar. He opened all the windows and painted the kitchen and got rid of her bed, and from then on he didn't seem to notice the house any more although he kept it scrupulously clean and tidy and took his sheets and towels to the Washerama every Monday night.

As an Assistant Citizen Leader in charge of a dozen small boys, he had recently returned from a summer camping trip to Wales when there came a knock at his front door. He opened it, and held it close to his shoulder.

'Is this – are you Mr Amory Bell?'

The woman was small and very thin, with a ratlike face and fingers like little white claws. She was poorly dressed, and from the broken suitcase she carried he imagined her to be selling something.

'Are you Amory Bell?'

Unwillingly he nodded, and the woman dropped her suitcase with a thump and tried to put her arms round his neck. She began to cry, making a little shivery mewing sound.

'Oh Amory– Oh my darling little boy, it's me. I'm your very own *Mum!*'

The more he worried about it, the less could Oliver come to any firm conclusion about the meaning of Big Goodnight as provided by Alastair.

When he was feeling happy he was sometimes able to dismiss the things he had been told as a lot of stupid lies, but other times – a lot of other times – he found it quite easy to believe that grown ups might start making laws about having to kill yourself when you got old. After all, they had wars, and reason told him that grown ups must quite like killing each other sometimes or else they wouldn't do it. They wouldn't even want to watch it on TV.

He also thought a lot about the world getting more and more filled up with people, and if there really wasn't enough space or food it appealed to his child's sense of fair play that people should have to take turns of a strictly limited period. In which case, no one could really quibble at the idea of Granny giving up her bit to Humphrey, who hadn't had a proper turn at all yet.

But the worst times were at night, when comfortable fantasies about spacemen had given way to images of corpses and coffins; lying in the dark he would visualise his grandmother as a whiteclad spook floating round the landings and waiting to pounce on people from the shadows. Sometimes he could hear the sort of hollow moaning she would make, so clearly that he would have to put his head under the bedclothes. And then, smothering in the heat, he would start thinking about the worst part of all; the part about Them killing him if he gave away the secret of Big Goodnight. He wondered what method They would use to kill him and how much it would hurt, and when he remembered Alastair saying that he was only in danger so long as doing away with old people was illegal, wished ignominiously that it would be made legal as soon as possible. And then hated himself for doing so. The nights were very long, and noticing his pale face and heavy eyes Willow gave him a herbal laxative.

The only person he could go to for assurance that it was all a game was Alastair himself, but it was now difficult to gain access to him because his auntie had arrived from America, a sun-dried woman with a big smile who wore safari suits and smoked yellow cigarettes. Among other presents she had brought Alastair a red baseball cap with an enormous peak which he wore all the time. He was very pompous and possessive about his auntie, and the baseball cap seemed somehow to have changed him from the old familiar fat nit into a cold and slightly menacing stranger.

No, Alastair was out, and there was no one else. He had no other close friends in the Young Citizens and shrank from approaching Nigel Schofield, whose elder brother had been the original source of information, because he and Nigel hadn't spoken since the time Nigel pinched Paul Clements' stamp album and blamed the theft on Oliver. He didn't like Nigel yet could draw only minimal comfort from the thought that as a transgressor in his own right, he must already be on the hit-list.

And because of their power and their unpredictability grown ups were out too, but as the warm summer days crept by it occurred to him that there was at least one positive step he could take. He could warn his grandmother of the fate rumoured to be in store for those of sixty and over, without necessarily telling her all the details. Pleased with the idea, he went up to the granny flat after school for the first time in two weeks.

She was delighted to see him, but he was so busy rehearsing what he was going to say that he forgot to return her greeting. He forgot to smile. He just stood there swinging his satchel by its strap and staring out through the window.

'Let's make some tea.'

She moved away to the kitchen and at first he wanted to say no thank you because the reason for his visit had taken away the old easy pleasure of being with her. He didn't even like being in the flat any more.

'How's Alastair?'

'Okay.'

'School going well?'

'Uh-huh.'

He didn't refuse lemonade and biscuits after all, but he didn't flop down on the carpet in the old casual, untidy way. He just sat on the edge of the chair and nibbled one biscuit while once again he assembled the words he was going to say.

'It won't be long before you go to camp now, will it?'

'No.'

'Looking forward to it?'

'Mmm.'

'Alastair going too?'

''spect so.'

He wished she'd shut up so that he could get the words right. She had stopped stirring her tea, and although he wasn't looking at her he could feel her looking across at him. He could feel that it was a kind and rather puzzled look.

'Oliver, is anything wrong?'

'No.' He drew a deep breath. 'It's just that I've come...' Then his courage failed him. 'Why?'

'Why? Well, you haven't been to see me for so long. And now you seem rather quiet and far away.'

'No, I'm not.'

'Have another biscuit.'

'No, thank you.'

It was far more difficult than he had thought. Twice he cleared his throat and then couldn't remember the opening words he had planned. It was like having to stand up and recite at school.

'Shall I make some coconut pyramids for when you go to camp?'

She was looking at him so brightly and affectionately with her head on one side that he couldn't stand it any more. He jumped up from the chair and began to speak very quickly.

'No, thank you. I just came to say that you mustn't let on to everybody when you're sixty. It's not certain yet but something very bad and horrible could happen, so you mustn't go telling all sorts of people *outside*.' He went quickly towards the door, his tongue wagging anxiously across his lips.

'Oliver,' she suppressed an involuntary giggle, 'what on earth do you mean?'

'It's a secret, so I can't tell you any more.'

'Is it a game?' Although still smiling, she now looked distinctly perplexed.

'No,' he said, 'it isn't a game. At least, it might be – but if it isn't they're planning to – well, they're planning to do something awful to – to some special sorts of people–'

All the right words, the words he had planned, had deserted him. Red-faced and mortified he grabbed at his satchel and bounded away down the stairs, banging the front door behind him.

He had tried to warn her but had made a muck of it. Illogically, it made him feel even more angry with her than he was with himself.

When Amory Bell's mother first returned, standing drab and unheralded on the doorstep that day, he had taken it for granted that she was merely paying him a visit, or at the very worst had come for the night, for even before they had had a chance to become re-acquainted he had no interest in her. Not even a tremor of idle curiosity. Once over the initial shock of her identity he provided her with a meal in the way he might have offered a saucerful of scraps to a stray cat, and hesitated visibly when she asked which room would be hers.

He asked how long she would be staying, and his marked lack of warmth caused her to look harassed and fidgety and to say that she didn't know. There were one or two things she had to sort out.

'But where have you come from? Where's your home?'

She shrugged. 'It's a long story.'

And I don't want to hear it, his expression told her.

'Oh Amory, can you remember the lovely old days when we three were all together, me and your Dad doing our act and you toddling about...' She began to cry.

'No. I was too young.'

'But you didn't come here until you were five.'

'This is all I remember.'

This was all he had any intention of remembering, for if there was any lingering memory of the old laughter and the warmth of kisses, he had long ago lost any desire to revive it.

'Oh Amory, you've grown into such a cold boy! You've grown cold just like your Gran.' And her tears fell like his had done on the terrible day when they abandoned him.

'There's another bed upstairs,' he said. 'But it's not very comfortable.'

'By the way–' she looked round the kitchen through blurred eyes,' where is Gran?'

'She's dead.'

'Oh dear. Oh, poor old soul.' Then she brightened. 'Well, if you're all on your own, you poor boy, you'll need someone to look after you, won't you?'

'I'm quite capable of looking after myself, thank you. The bed's in the small back bedroom and the blankets are in the cupboard.' He shunted her towards the door. 'Goodnight.'

She had been staying in the house for a week before she confessed that she was homeless. That she had no friends and hardly any money.

'Wasn't there another man after my father?'

'Which – how did you know?'

'You brought him here once.'

'Did I? Well, we came unstuck and he went

back to Ireland.'

'I see.'

'Oh Amory, you used to love me so much when you were a little boy, but I sometimes feel you don't love me at all now.'

The intervening years had not been kind to her, and the laughing lively girl with the springy curls he used to try to unwind had become old and sunken, with a peevish whine and little claw hands that were always trying to hook themselves on to him. She spent most mornings in bed, and in the afternoons sat about in a grubby old house-coat trimmed with white maribou which made her look like a moulting hen. The main business of the day was a totter to the off-licence for a half bottle of gin.

To begin with, the discovery that she drank spirits appalled Amory almost as much as her presence in his life, and still imbued with some of the deeper tones of old Gran's chapelism he sought to dissuade her – confiscating the bottles sometimes openly, sometimes by stealth, and seeking to replace the noxious stuff with the healthy innocence of Ovaltine or Bovril.

'I can't – I can't, it'll make me fat–'

'Don't be crazy. You're as thin as a stick.'

'But fat girls are unattractive.' A pout, a flutter of decaying feathers. 'You don't like fat girls, do you, Amory?'

'I haven't much time to spare for girls, fat

or thin.'

'Oh Amory, you're not trying to tell me that you're–'

'No, of course I'm not.' But despite the truth of his words, his heart would sink at the dirty little gleam that would light the corners of her eyes.

'There *is* something funny about you, Amory. Anybody who likes being with little boys instead of going out with girls is very funny, to my way of thinking.'

'When it comes to thinking,' he would say, taut with suppressed fury, 'I think you'd better keep quiet.'

'Oh, *Amory*–' a quick collapse into tears – 'fancy talking to your Mum like that! Your poor old Mum who loves you although anyone can see you don't love her.'

Once or twice he even tried to say that he loved her too, in the hope of keeping the peace. But the word love refused to form on his tongue; back in the old days when he had known the meaning of it he had not known the word, and then afterwards, in his Gran's way of expressing things, the word love had been vetoed and had gradually come to mean something dirty like brassière or french letter.

'I'm fond of you,' he would mutter untruthfully.

'Fond, fond,' she would jeer. 'What good's that to anybody? I bet you're more than fond of your nasty little boys.'

116

So he would walk out, and she would reach for the gin bottle.

He never returned home after work without a faint gleam of hope that he would find her gone; that the gin bottles, the dirty bits of feathers and all her other dreary impedimenta would have vanished, leaving the house tidy, clean and cold the way he liked it. But she was always there, crouching over the fire half-asleep if drunk, or reading teenage love stories if sober.

'I'm cooking some fish for supper. Do you want any?'

'What sort is it?'

'Smoked haddock.'

'No, I don't feel well enough. Oh Amory, you'll never know what I've been through – some of it was my own fault, I know, but not all of it. Other girls don't have such lousy tricks played on them by such lousy men–'

'You'd better eat something. Looks as if you've had nothing all day.'

'I'm not hungry. I've got out of the way of eating.'

'Please yourself.'

He set about preparing his meal, warming the plate on top of the pan in which the fish was poaching, then cutting some slices of bread and butter. There was neat economy in every movement.

'Are you going out again tonight, Amory?'

'Yes.'

'To this Young Citizen thing? Why ever do you let it take up so much of your time?'

'Because it's one of the very few things I believe in,' he said.

'I think I'll go and lie down, I don't feel well.'

She trailed out, and sitting on the edge of the small truckle bed reached for her suitcase and the bottle hidden inside. She drank herself to sleep.

And so they both settled into some hopeless kind of half-life. Every now and then she would pull herself together and insist that she was going to do the housekeeping; that she would clean the house and cook for him, but on the evening he returned to find the kitchen curtains on fire he told her quite categorically that she only remained in the house on condition that she left the entire running of it to him. The chill dislike with which he spoke prompted another gush of tears and a threat to do away with herself since no one loved her any more.

And that was her trouble. No one had ever seemed capable of loving her for more than a limited time. Sooner or later they all grew indifferent to her, and the more desperately she wheedled and giggled and pouted, the more surely their indifference hardened into disgust. She learned to recognise it in their eyes, this death of the great romance that had its roots in music hall love songs and cheap boardinghouse bedrooms. Coming unstuck, she always called it, and the last time it happened was every bit as painful as the first.

She had been on her own for three months after the end of the last great love when it suddenly occurred to her that the world in its infinite wisdom has more than one sort of love to offer. What about the sacred love that exists between a mother and her child?

She dried her eyes, and from that moment on it seemed as if Amory had never been out of her thoughts; as if she had been hovering over his shoulder like some watchful guardian angel during all the time while he struggled with his funny little problems at school and at home with his Gran. She thought with increasing tenderness about him growing to maturity; getting hair down below and talking in a man's voice and then one day meeting her in some nice place somewhere and looking her over with a man's appreciative eyes. But Amory, my *dear*, she would say, I'm your *mother!* And they would both laugh their heads off and be able to love one another for ever and ever with a pure wonderful love that had something religious about it as well as a pleasant little tingle of you-know-what.

But it hadn't worked. And this pale quiet man who was still living alone in the same house after all these years looked at her with a cold aversion that destroyed the last sad little remnants of her just as surely as if he had stamped on a butterfly.

Despite the débâcle with his grandmother Oliver was still deeply concerned about the question of Big Goodnight. Sometimes he believed in it and sometimes he didn't, but whichever way his opinion happened to be facing he was beginning to find the idea of legal disposal of elderly people less and less disturbing. His mind no long shuddered over the horrors of his grandmother as a spook, but rather over the horrors of a world where no one had enough room to move. He pictured it filled with rank upon rank of skeleton figures standing rigidly to attention for year after year without even enough space to fall down when they fainted. He didn't want it to be like that.

The week before they went to camp he was one of the volunteers helping to pack and stow gear in readiness in the church hall and when it was all finished and the others had gone home he walked quietly up behind Mr Bell, drew a deep decisive breath and said: 'Excuse me, Mr Bell, but is there really such a thing as B–'

But he got it wrong again, because he made Mr Bell jump and that had the effect of making him cross. He turned round on Oliver like a whiplash.

'What are you doing, still hanging about?

You should have been home ages ago.'

The shock, and the awful unfairness towards someone who had been a voluntary helper, stung Oliver badly. His eyes filled with tears and his ears felt as if they would burst into flame. He turned away.

'Sorry.'

But Mr Bell, with a pencil stuck behind his ear, went over to him and put a hand on his shoulder.

'Now then, what's up, hey?'

'Nun – nothing.'

'In that case, there's no point in getting in a stew, is there?'

The genial sympathy after his previous sharpness made Oliver want to cry even more, but he sniffed and snuffled his way back to coherence while Mr Bell waited patiently.

'Okay now?'

'Uh-huh.'

'Sure nothing's wrong?'

Oliver shook his head, but instead of telling him to cut off home, Mr Bell walked with him across the deserted hall. They sat on the edge of the stage with their feet dangling.

'Things used to get me down sometimes when I was your age,' Mr Bell said. 'Generally it was a combination of little things rather than one great big one. And it would have made it much easier if I could have talked to someone about it.'

121

'Couldn't you?' Oliver was sufficiently composed now to be able to stare at him.

'No, not really.'

'I get fed up sometimes,' Oliver said companionably. 'But it doesn't last long.'

'Everything okay at home?'

'Uh-huh.'

'Parents pleased you're coming away to camp with us?'

'Uh-huh.'

'That's good.'

'My grandmother's pleased, too.'

Although the moment had passed when he could have asked about Big Goodnight, there was no difficulty in mentioning his grandmother's name; in dropping the word into the conversation as one would drop a stone into a pond to test its depth.

'Fine.' Mr Bell's tone was equable enough, but the slight stiffening of his lips didn't escape Oliver, who was now staring at his profile with frank curiosity. The tears might have belonged to yesterday.

'My grandmother's quite nice, really.'

'Mmm.'

'I mean, some boys' grandmothers are horrible. They don't like you jumping about and making a row, but mine's okay. And she can make nice cakes – the sort we don't have at home because they're not healthy.'

'Nothing wrong with the odd slice of cake, but too much of anything can be bad for you.'

'Uh-huh. And she's going to be sixty when we get back from camp.'

Oliver waited expectantly. He no longer wanted to ask about Big Goodnight because it was becoming more fun to tiptoe round the subject. Nightmares forgotten, it was like playing an interesting game, and with wide clear eyes he continued to observe Mr Bell's profile. It remained stony.

'Somebody said I shouldn't have brought my grandmother to the concert that time.'

'Oh? Who was it?'

'I've forgotten.'

'Did they tell you why?'

Mr Bell turned to look at him, and Oliver's newly-found self confidence began to lose height. His ears started glowing again, as if they were becoming ignited by the intensity of Mr Bell's pale stare. There was something terrible about his stare.

'No.'

'Did you ask?'

'Yes – no ... I don't think so.'

'Because only very stupid people talk about things they don't understand. The rest of us wait until someone who really knows about the subject is ready to explain it carefully and sensibly so that we won't get hold of the wrong end of the stick and start making fools of ourselves in front of other people. Don't you agree?'

'Yes.' Bereft now of all confidence, Oliver could only wriggle and dwindle down into himself. He gazed at his fingers.

'So I suggest that you pass that message on to whoever tried to stuff you up with a lot of silly nonsense. Off you go now.'

The interview was over and Oliver departed, confused and shamefaced, yet with a curiously light heart. It sounds as if Big Goodnight had only been a game after all and he looked forward to punching Alastair right in the middle of his stupid baseball cap next time he saw him.

Instead of going straight home he walked to the end of Bridge Road and then turned down into the long narrow alleyway that led towards the river and the field of council allotments. If his father was working there he could cadge a lift home with him, but in any case he always enjoyed the alleyway because it was dank-smelling and secretive and over-hung with trees and hedges through which he could spy into the neglected bottom ends of gardens. A lot of them only had bonfires and compost heaps and greenhouses, but a couple had old air raid shelters, grey sinister windowless buildings half-buried in summer foliage that interested him very much. He thought how enjoyable the war must have been, then remembered that wars were wicked and undesirable.

He saw his father's car parked at the

entrance to the allotments and found him hoeing a row of vegetables, gently nudging the little weeds aside as if he were reluctant to practise any form of discrimination.

He smiled when he saw Oliver. 'Come to help?'

'Uh-huh. What are these little feathery things?'

'Carrots. They grow underground.'

'How d'you know when they're done?'

'You have to pull one up and see.'

'Shall we pull one up now?'

'Can do.'

Oliver pulled, then sat back on his heels considering the small orange-coloured sprout to which the soil still clung.

'It's got a hole in it.'

'Probably a mouse has taken a bite.'

'I thought mice ate cheese.'

'They'll eat anything if they're hungry. Paper and wood, if there's nothing better.'

'Would we eat paper and wood if we were hungry?'

'We'd have to be pretty desperate.'

'But just supposing we were. I mean, supposing the world does get fuller and fuller of people so there isn't enough of anything to go round – what'll we do?'

'We mustn't let it get to that state,' his father said. 'Long, long before then we've got to think up various ways of making sure that there aren't more people than the earth can provide for.'

'How will we?'

'Oh, there are lots and lots of ways. One of them for instance is to persuade people not to have so many babies. In the meantime, it's beginning to get dark and Mummy'll be wondering where we are. Let's pick a nice big bundle of spinach to take home for her.'

They picked it in silence, the crisp leaves squeaking as they were pulled. They stuffed them into a big nylon net from the toolshed that his father shared with someone else's father who grew vegetables without chemicals, and then they drove home.

Halfway down the road in which they lived Seth suddenly braked sharply, jumped from the car and ran towards a small moving shape lying close to the gutter. The dipped headlights shimmered on his bent back and Oliver watched, motionless, as he slowly stood up and came towards the car with the thing held outstretched in his hands.

'Quick – is the rug on the back seat?'

Oliver grabbed it up in a bunch.

'Fold it flat on your knees – open the door–'

His father came round to the rear door of the car and placed the cat very gently on Oliver's lap. It made a useless little movement with its head and shoulders and then lay still.

'It's been run over, we'd better take it home.'

They drove very slowly in second gear and the warmth of the cat's living body penetrated the folds of the rug and warmed Oliver's knees. His hand hovered about its head, anxious to caress it.

'Oh, poor thing, does it hurt it? Will it die?'

'I expect it's in a certain amount of pain, but I don't suppose it'll die. We'll get the vet to take a look at it.'

They turned in at the gateway, Oliver wincing as the car slowly jolted over a pothole. As instructed, he remained in his seat while his father went to the garage to find a large cardboard box. With infinite care he transferred the cat and the rug to it and then carried it indoors, Oliver close to his side.

'Poor thing's been run over, we saw it lying at the side of the road—'

'It wasn't you who did it?' For a second, accusation sparkled in Willow's small eyes.

'Oh, gosh no – Daddy was just—'

'No, I just caught sight of it as I was driving past. Some callous swine must have hit it and just not bothered—'

'Perhaps they didn't see it—'

'Maybe not, but they'd have felt the *bump.*'

They laid the box on the floor close to the Aga, and Oliver watched with his tongue wagging rapidly to and fro as his parents knelt to examine the animal. Once again it struggled to sit up, and this time almost managed it before slumping back again. It looked round vaguely, and gave a little mew.

'Poor old boy, poor little kitty, where does it hurt, then? What a rotten thing to happen.'

Tenderly and compassionately their fingers explored the cat's body, hoping to deduce broken bones from any unusual protuberances. There was no blood. Willow stroked its head.

'Poor little cat. Never mind, we'll make you better.'

'Looks like a stray,' Seth said. 'It's terribly thin and I think it's got mange.'

'My God, it makes me so angry, the way living things get treated,' Willow said in a low bitter voice. 'Somebody probably had it as a dear little fluffy kitten and then threw it out when it got big and boring.'

'I don't think cats are boring when they're big,' Oliver said eagerly. 'Can we keep it for ours?'

'We've got to get it well again first,' his father said, tucking the rug protectively round it. 'Get a saucer of milk for it and see if it can drink.'

Oliver flew to the fridge and poured the cream from the top of a new bottle of milk. He stirred in some sugar with his finger.

At first the saucer seemed to fill the cat with alarm; its eyes became huge and black and it struggled feebly to get away. Then it relaxed, sniffed at the milk and made a half-hearted attempt to lap, before turning its head aside.

'It's still too dazed. It's suffering from shock.'

'Will it get better?'

'Yes, darling, I expect so. We must just let it rest peacefully–'

'Can't we get the vet?'

'It's too late now, he'll have gone home. But we'll take it to the surgery first thing tomorrow if it isn't any better.'

'Promise?'

'Of course we promise.'

Oliver waited with his parents as the cat's eyes began to close, and when it gave a sigh and laid its chin on a convenient fold in the rug each of them felt as if a small victory had been achieved.

'Rest and warmth is all it wants.'

'Just let it lie there and recover in peace.'

Carefully Seth screened the box from the light, and with both his parents moving quietly and speaking in hushed voices, Oliver decided on impulse to slip up to the granny flat with the news that a stray cat had been run over but was getting better now and they were going to keep it.

'Oh, thank goodness you found it!' Her eyes shone. It was the first time he had been to see her since the bungled attempt to warn her about Big Goodnight.

'Yes. I've got to go now.'

'Already? You've only just come.'

'I know. But I'm busy.'

Without looking at her he sidled out of the door and ran away. Whether Big Goodnight was only a game or whether it wasn't, its poison was already at work.

The thought of the cat drove sleep away that night, and Oliver lay in the summer darkness remembering the warmth of its body on his lap in the car and the beaten look in its eyes as it refused the saucer of milk.

Two years ago he had had a hamster, but although he enjoyed holding it and letting it sniff him it had never really done much, and he had felt no more than a passing regret when it escaped. Sometimes he had wanted to be like Alastair and have a dog but his parents gently discouraged the idea; dogs were dirty, rather sordid animals, whose faeces gave people diseases. But now they had the cat, and he glowed at the thought of them all combining their efforts to take care of it and nurse it back to health.

He wondered what the cat was doing now. Alone in the kitchen, it was probably feeling a bit fed up. Supposing it wanted to lap some milk and couldn't reach the saucer? Supposing it was in pain and couldn't make anyone hear?

He scrambled out of bed, and with the aid

of his torch crept silently downstairs.

The cat was still in the basket and appeared to be lying in the same position. Disturbed by the beam of light it raised its chin and attempted a faint miaow. Sinking down beside it Oliver stroked the top of its head and then let his fingers play gently round the curves of its ears. Under the fur he could feel hard scaly lumps and wondered what they were.

To his great delight it attempted to drink a little milk, raising itself painfully on its front legs while Oliver tilted the saucer solicitously. When it lay back again he could have sworn he recognised affection glowing in its eyes. He sat stroking it for a little while longer and then glided back to bed, certain that he would never feel like this about two little Ugandans.

And in the morning the cat was sitting up trying to wash itself.

'All it needs is a chance to recover,' Willow said. 'We must buy it something nice to eat because it does look so dreadfully thin.'

'What shall we call it?' Spooning up cornflakes Oliver watched the cat lovingly.

'Anything you like,' his father said. 'How about Hilary? That'd do for a boy or a girl.'

'No,' Oliver said. 'Elderberry.'

'Elderberry? Why Elderberry?'

'I just like the word.'

So the cat became Elderberry, and

although it didn't seem inclined to move very much, or to eat more than a mouthful of the food they prepared for it, it purred whenever they went near.

Gently, very gently, Seth tried to set it on its feet, supporting it under its belly while Willow and Oliver crooned encouragement, but although the cat seemed to want to please them it fell sideways as soon as the supporting hand was withdrawn.

'We'll let the vet look at him tomorrow morning,' his parents said, and Oliver snatched impatiently at Humphrey, who kept crawling towards the cat's box.

'Go somewhere else, you thick *nit!*'

'Don't be impatient with him, Oliver. He's only a baby and he needs to experiment.'

'Well, I don't want him experimenting near Elderberry.'

'He only wants to look at him, and we do all want to share him, don't we?'

Grudgingly, Oliver supposed that they did.

The morning they took Elderberry to the vet was the day school broke up for the summer holidays. They didn't do any proper lessons and they had ice cream and strawberries, and on the way home Alastair, who was still wearing his baseball cap, tore open his school report and read it.

'Open yours too, go on.'

Oliver demurred.

132

'Scared of your parents?'

'No.'

'Go on then, open it. I dare you!'

Oliver walked on in silence. He didn't want to open his school report because it wasn't addressed to him and upbringing had already instilled in him a healthy respect for other people's private property. His parents rarely scrutinised things belonging to him without invitation.

'You're scared.'

'No, I'm not.'

'Why don't you open it then?'

Abruptly Oliver stopped dead, and stood glaring at Alastair's derisive face sheltered under the huge red peak. 'Because I can't be *bothered*,' he said, and marched off without him.

When he reached home he went straight to the kitchen, and the first thing he saw was the empty box down by the Aga. He rushed to find his parents.

'Where's Elderberry? What's happened to Elderberry?'

Willow came out of the big room they used as an office. 'Now listen, Oliver,' she said very quietly and seriously, 'I'm afraid that Elderberry's gone.'

'Where's he gone? What for?'

She tried to draw him to her. He felt her thin ribs pressing against his face, then Seth appeared. Oliver wrenched himself away.

'Where's Elderberry?'

'He's with the vet,' his father said. 'Now come and sit down because I want to talk to you as if you were grown up.'

They went back into the office.

'Elderberry's dead, isn't he?'

'Yes.'

'But he was getting *better!*'

Sorrowfully his father shook his head. 'No, not really, and the vet discovered that his back was injured. It wasn't hurting him, I promise you there was no pain, and the vet said he could have operated and made it all right again, but he also discovered that Elderberry was too old. He was a very old cat, and he probably hadn't got much longer to live anyway. He'd also got mange, and the vet and I talked it over and decided that the kindest thing we could possibly do would be to put him to sleep.'

'You mean kill him?'

'No, I don't.' His father spoke with emphasis. 'Putting to sleep is quite different from killing. Killing is something generally done in hatred or in a rage, and is wicked, but putting an animal to sleep when it's old and ill is a gentle loving act. Whatever happens, you must learn the difference between the two.'

'It was no more than saying goodnight to him, really,' Willow said.

It was a miserable shame about the cat –

they had both been close to tears earlier in the day – but even so Willow and Seth were totally unprepared for Oliver's reaction.

Wild and white-faced he turned round on them and screamed: 'You're pigs! You're both pigs!' before hurling himself out through the door into the courtyard. Tears were choking him, convulsing him in huge heartbroken spasms when he cannoned violently into his grandmother. Her hands found his shoulders, gripped them tightly and then folded over them like a pair of strong protective wings.

'Oliver, I'm so deeply sorry.'

For an instant he sought relief in the warm darkness of her dress then snatched himself away. Grief became rage, and fresh burning tears blinded his eyes and poured down his cheeks. His voice could only come in a series of high staccato hiccups.

'It's all because of you! I hate you! I wish you hadn't come!'

He didn't know what he meant. He could only try to shriek out at last, and as if in protest, against all the conflict and confusion that had plagued him over the last few weeks.

She let him go, and watched helplessly as he rushed like a mad thing out into the tangled garden.

'Leave him to his grief.' Seth put his arm round her. 'And don't take any notice of the things he said.'

Although she was a drunkard, Amory Bell's mother showed no sign of dying in the foreseeable future. Neither did she show any sign of wishing to go and live somewhere else.

Once or twice he suggested that she might like to rent a couple of rooms on her own so that she could be a bit more independent, but the idea seemed to fill her with terror. She would be so lonely, so defenceless, and she wouldn't be able to stand the nights. She no longer asked anything of life except to be with her boy, whom she loved and cherished in the way she knew that he really loved and cherished her.

'You do love me, don't you, Amory?'

'We're not really talking about love, we're talking about what's the best thing to do.'

'Because I love you. I'm so proud of you, and if you didn't let me live here with you I'd just do away with myself–'

'I think you'd be much happier looking after yourself in a nice little place of your own–'

'You see darling, let's be honest – I *had* you, didn't I? And nobody can really understand how a mother feels about someone who was in her tum for nine whole months. Oh, it was such a *happy* time, Amory...'

The moment she started on the wonders of motherhood he had difficulty in concealing his loathing of her. It twisted his mouth

136

and glistened in his eyes, this squeamish abhorrence, this hatred of something that was essentially dirty and ugly, stupid and banal. He hated to touch her, as he hated to touch anyone else, even by accident.

The solution to the burden of her presence came to him gradually, and once assured that it was a viable proposition he went about the necessary arrangements in a quiet and systematic fashion. He began by opening the old suitcase under the truckle bed one Saturday evening when she had gone down to the off-licence, and forcing himself to delve among the tubes of sticky make-up and bits of soiled underwear until he came to the old chocolate box crammed with letters, photographs and old theatre programmes. *Frankie & Johnnie, Sophisticated Entertainers from London's West End,* and beneath it the smudgily reproduced picture of a sly, snappily dressed man and a pretty pouting girl wearing a hat with what looked like a lot of paper roses on it; he flicked it aside, together with letters signed by 'Your ever loving Harry', 'Yours till the pips squeak, Joey', and 'I kiss your Darling Lips, always, Monty'.

He found some blurred snapshots of a tiny boy standing laughingly to attention with a seaside bucket and spade which he also laid aside, and when he came to her marriage certificate he learned that she had originally been Frances Maude Skinner and that she

137

must have been thirty-eight when he was born.

Which meant that she was now sixty-three. However repugnant he found her he was surprised that she should be so old, and tucking the certificate into his wallet he thought fleetingly of a woman well past the prime child-bearing years having to struggle with pregnancy and the need to look like a primped up chorus girl. It must have been hard, but it was no affair of his, and he shovelled the rest of the contents back into the chocolate box, replaced it in the suitcase and then pushed it under the mean little bed with a sigh of relief.

Two days later he called at the Ministry of Social Security on her behalf, then took the following day off work and travelled by train to the southern side of London and applied for a job as a general electrician. He got one, and because his prospective employer liked his neat appearance and quiet demeanour, he recommended a furnished room with a nice old couple called Krasnor who had a small jeweller's shop not far away.

The next thing of vital importance was to transfer his assistant leadership of the Ilford Young Citizens to a branch nearer his new area and this was achieved with equal facility, plus an unexpected promotion to full Citizen Leader. The branch was a newly formed one, and needed the creative inspiration of an especially keen type, they said.

So he was all set up. Nothing remained but to give in his notice at the old shop where he had worked since leaving school. He stayed until the end of the following week and gravely accepted the ten pounds and paper-back copy of *The Modern Electrician's Handbook* which they gave him as a leaving present.

Looking round the old house where he had spent the greater part of his life he found few things that he needed to take with him. His clothes, his backpack camping equipment, one or two reference books and some papers connected with the Young Citizens, and that was all. There were no friends to say goodbye to, and the neighbours had long ago accepted that the quiet young Mr Bell preferred people to mind their own business and leave him alone.

On the evening before he left he made a macaroni cheese and persuaded his mother to share a little of it. The remainder he covered over with greaseproof paper and put in the larder for her, together with half a pound of sausages, a small brown loaf and a new packet of butter. For a moment he had toyed with the idea of buying her a whole bottle of gin, then dismissed it as an unwarrantable cynicism.

Yet he had no tremor of pity for her, not even a moment's curiosity to know how she would fare on her own. After her customary trip to the off-licence (*A little fresh air helps me to sleep, darling*), she went up to bed and he went to his own room about an hour later, having wound the kitchen clock and left a small pile of silver for the gas meter. Once during the night he heard her cry out as if in some sort of anguish, but when he paused to listen outside her door at breakfast time on the following morning he could hear the sound of snoring. She rarely awoke before eleven.

He made a cup of tea, ate a slice of bread, and then leaving her claim form for Supplementary Benefit in a prominent position on the table, he left the house. Having closed the door quietly with the aid of his latch key he dropped it back through the letterbox. He left by bicycle, his belongings packed in two canvas panniers, and he turned the corner of the road without glancing back.

He had been living at the Krasnors' for almost a year when the plainclothes man called on him with the information that a Mrs Frances Maude Bell, believed to be his mother, had been found dead in bed at an address in Ilford. The house was neglected, the body in an emaciated condition, but foul play was not suspected.

So it was all over and done with, and now there were no more decaying old women who could possibly encroach upon his privacy.

Or so it seemed. But the long years had had their effect, and although he was happy to the point of quiet exultancy in his new life, he found that he had not escaped as completely as he had envisaged. Because the world was still full of old woman, and old men too, shambling past him in the streets and shuffling about in the supermarket. And they came into the shop where he worked, asking him to mend pre-transistor radios and to put new elements in old kettles that leaked. He tried to treat them with kindness but the words wouldn't come, any more than he could force a cheerful smile. He loathed them all, quite impartially, and his loathing was increased when he read a new Government report on the rapidly increasing life-span of the average British citizen. A combination of welfare state and medical science seemed all set to ensure that people never died at all, but were to be kept dribbling on into senility at the expense of the young, who would have both to nurse them and earn the money with which to keep them. It seemed as if the exceptional horror of his own youth would become the normal pattern unless something was done to prevent it.

It was a grotesque situation and for a while he toyed with the idea of joining – or perhaps even forming – some sort of movement dedicated to a more rational approach to old age, but always drew back at the thought of the publicity, not to mention notoriety, that inevitably went these days with nailing one's colours to the mast. His own natural preference was for action by stealth.

He came upon the perfect alternative one Sunday morning when he was searching through his file of papers connected with the Young Citizens. He found what he was looking for, but continued to wander back over old letters and bulletins from headquarters until he came to the printed manifesto which set out the aims and aspirations of the organisation.

Every boy was given one on being formally accepted into his local group, and although Amory had long known them all by heart, the wording of the last clause but one had temporarily slipped his memory.

We believe in the dignity of life;
In showing kindness and consideration to
  those about us
Whatever their race or creed.
We believe in the beauty of life;
And when it draws towards its natural close
We will relinquish it with grace.

There surely was the answer. And his mission in life as teacher and initiator was at last dazzlingly clear.

PART TWO

'Of course, we don't regard ourselves as an elderly group *primarily*,' said the woman who was sitting on Mrs Dansie's sofa. 'We prefer to think of ourselves as a little coterie of music-loving folk who happen to be retired.'

'It sounds delightful.'

'And having heard that you had recently moved into the vicinity – what a talented couple your dear young souls appear to be – I wanted to welcome you and express the hope on behalf of us all that you will join us at some of our evenings.'

The woman was of shapely but commodious build, wearing a silk summer dress and a straw hat trimmed with artificial cherries. The hat was something of a surprise in an age when few elderly women aspired to more than a careful pastel-rinsed perm, and it shaded the smooth pale skin and calm immobile features so that the overall effect was vaguely discomforting to Mrs Dansie, who had been woken from a siesta. Feeling warm and dishevelled she gathered herself discreetly together, then smiled and thanked the woman for her kind thoughtfulness.

'I myself was on the platform in my youth,'

the woman continued, and Mrs Dansie produced another smile and asked in what capacity.

'I sang mezzo with the D'Oyly Carte until marriage claimed me. My darling was a flautist.'

Was, noted Mrs Dansie. She said. 'Mine was a dental surgeon.'

'And you lost him only recently, I gather?'

'Last autumn.'

'Ambrose was gathered up more than six years ago.'

So where does that leave us? wondered Mrs Dansie. I hope we're not going to sit and compare notes.

'How very sad,' she said courteously.

The woman had arrived uninvited and unannounced. Her name was Mrs Portman-Ayres and Mrs Dansie remembered having seen and heard her shopping in the local delicatessen. She decided that the fact was too trivial to mention.

'I expect you are fond of music, aren't you?'

There was a faint hint of menace in Mrs Portman-Ayres' tone, as if challenging Mrs Dansie to admit that she voted other than Conservative.

'I'm fond of *Porgy and Bess*,' Mrs Dansie said bravely, 'but I can't honestly claim to have much knowledge of the technical side of music.'

'My dear, you don't have to!' Mrs Port-man-Ayres laughed without disturbing her features. 'All we ask is that you sit back and enjoy yourself. After all, that's what life is about at our age, isn't it?'

Mrs Dansie agreed that it was, and suddenly warming to her guest invited her to stay for some tea but Mrs Portman-Ayres rose to her feet with protestations about being unable to spare the time.

'My dear, I have a million and one things to do, and I'm sure you have too. But if you could spare the time to come to our small recital on the fifteenth – here is my card with the address – we should be more than delighted to welcome you. Seven-thirty would not be too early?'

Mrs Dansie said that it wouldn't, and thanked her again. Mrs Portman-Ayres sailed towards the head of the staircase, then paused to look round.

'Such a sensible little house. A bijou residence is all we really require at our stage in life.'

'Goodbye,' Mrs Dansie said. 'And thank you so much for calling.'

On her own again she wandered round the room plumping up cushions and tweaking at the bowl of roses on the coffee table. It was very kind of this Mrs Portman-Ayres to have taken the trouble to call, and she was grateful, while remaining dubious about the possibility of making friends; she sensed that it would take more than music and widowhood to unite them.

However, thought Mrs Dansie, wandering out onto the balcony, it wouldn't do me any harm to go to her thingummy. It might even do me some good.

For several weeks now she had been aware of a slight sense of letdown so far as her new lifestyle was concerned. Although independent by nature she had somehow envisaged meeting more people and being just a shade more a part of the bustling life outside the granny flat. Willow and Seth had their own lives to lead and she had no particular desire to be the only grandmother twinkling cosily in a group of rather earnest young parents, but... She leaned over the balustrade and looked down into the hot, still garden.

Social barriers were supposed to have crumbled, but now and then she had an irrational feeling that other obstacles were being erected in their place; as if there was a deliberate policy afoot to organise everyone within a designated age area, starting with playgroups, sub-teen culture, teenage clans and then young wives' clubs, parents' associations and so on down the line until one reached – she drew a deep breath – Mrs Portman-Ayres' little coterie of music-loving folk who happened to be retired.

Depression descended. The oblique reference to Bertie had upset her and she wondered what he was doing now. It would be nice to think that he was filling cavities in the teeth of the Almighty, for Bertie hated to be idle, but technology had obliterated the old familiar folklore of a life hereafter and offered no form of consolation in its place. All she had was the final memory of electronic music leading him down to a precision-built furnace.

But the real cause of her depression was Oliver. He had been at camp for several days now and each morning she awoke with the hope that there might be a postcard from him. But none came, and as the morning wore on she would become increasingly conscious of the miserable apprehensions caused by his change of attitude. Again and again she traced the course of their relationship, lingering over the memory of early constraint melting into laughter over jokes and riddles and then the slow and inexplicable deterioration; the helpless awareness on her part that their easy camaraderie was becoming obscured by a cloud of evasion, diffidence and awkward self-consciousness until it exploded on that terrible afternoon when he first learned that the stray cat had been put to sleep.

It's all because of you! I hate you! I wish you hadn't come here!

The words still seared her, but as the first

shock of them had begun to subside a little she had tried to comfort herself with the theory that Oliver might have been brooding unhappily on the prospect of having to welcome two little Ugandan refugees; Willow and Seth in their praiseworthy desire to alleviate human suffering had perhaps been just a trace perfunctory in breaking the news, but that wasn't the reason for his change in attitude towards her and she knew it.

The real reason was something she couldn't get at, but it had something to do with her. And she couldn't get rid of the idea that it also had something to do with Mr Bell.

Mr Bell of the nondescript features and pale eyes. She was curious to know more about him, and once or twice even toyed with the idea of asking him up for coffee one evening. The dispensation of a little gracious grandmotherly hospitality might well disarm him and make possible some kind of rapport between them which would be nice for Oliver's sake, yet she made no positive move. Although Oliver had told her where he lived she didn't know whether she would have to include a wife in the invitation, but the main reason for hesitating lay in the memory of their only previous meeting.

The sensation of evil that had afterwards jerked her from sleep was as vivid as ever, and she knew that she would never seek his friendship because he frightened her.

Instead, she was going to have a sensible chat with Oliver when he came home, and one of the things she was going to get clear was the meaning of this strange and garbled warning about something nasty happening to certain sorts of people.

Coming in from the balcony she decided to cheer herself up by writing to her sister, then changed her mind and went downstairs. She crossed the hot courtyard to the big house. Willow's car was in the garage but it was Seth whom she met in the hall.

'Hullo, Granny.'

'Hullo, dear. Sorry to barge in–'

'Not at all. Glad to see you.'

He stood waiting deferentially while a number of daft excuses for being there flashed through her mind. Please Seth there's a large spider in the bath, the fridge is making a funny noise, the phone won't work; but she didn't use any of them. Instead, she heard herself speak the truth. 'I just came over to see whether you've heard from Oliver yet.'

'Oh yes.' His smile was very white through the brown beard. 'We had a postcard this morning.'

'Is he all right? Enjoying himself, I mean?'

'Well, they'd only just arrived, but he sounded very happy and excited. They're camping in the grounds of a big house and they're allowed to swim in the lake.'

'I do hope it's safe–'

'Oh I'm sure it is. This chap who's in charge–'

'Mr Bell–'

'Mr Bell seems to have it all taped. With kids of that age it's a matter of winning their trust. Once you've earned that they'll obey you because they want to and not because they're afraid to do otherwise.'

'I suppose the Hitler Youth Movement started by winning their trust.' She didn't know what made her say that, and Seth's rather startled glance made her feel silly.

'I don't think an ecological movement could ever have much in common with fascism,' he said.

'No, of course not. I was only joking.' And to prove it, she laughed. 'When is he coming home, by the way?'

'In about another ten days, I think.'

'Oh, good. I feel a bit–'

She was going to make a joke about feeling lonely without him and then turn on her heel and walk away, but the phone rang in the office and without waiting to hear the rest of her remark Seth waved a friendly hand and went to answer it.

She returned to the granny flat wishing that she had been invited to read the postcard. But most of all she had wanted to ask Seth if he knew why Oliver had turned on her with such violence that day. Seth had been very kind to her and she could still remember the warmth of his arm round her shoulder, yet somehow it was impossible to reintroduce the subject.

She loved him as she loved Willow, but the sad truth was that she couldn't talk to either of them without feeling distinctly old and foolish.

'Now, who can tell me what this is?'

The beetle lay motionless on Mr Bell's hand. Only the design on its shell seemed to quiver in the sunlight dancing down through the trees.

'A cockchafer.'

'Rubbish, think again. How many stripes has it got?'

'Two.'

'Well, then.'

'It's a flea beetle!' The high little shriek came from Oliver Mitchell. With big teeth flashing and ears turning pink he looked round in triumph.

'Well done.' Carefully Mr Bell tipped the beetle from the palm of his hand onto the grass. 'All these creatures are at risk due to crop spraying, and if we're not careful they'll be wiped out completely. Which would be a pity, wouldn't it?'

'Yes!' they chorused, and watched it regain the power of movement and scuttle away. They followed Mr Bell out into the open parkland.

'At the same time we've got to try to pre-serve this thing called the balance of nature, which means not letting one type of living creature completely overwhelm another, so that its species becomes extinct.'

'Like dinosaurs,' someone suggested.

'Yes, although the reason for their dis-appearance has got more to do with the change in climate than being the victims of other predators. Guess who are the most ruthless predators on earth.'

Heat haze shimmered over the motionless chestnut trees that dotted the park. Grass-hoppers churred at their feet.

'Ants,' Alastair said.

'Sharks–'

'Wolves–'

'You're all wrong,' Mr Bell said. 'The most ruthless predators on earth are human beings. Us, in other words.'

Oliver rambled along in the rear, sucking a blade of grass while he considered the idea of being even nastier than a shark or a wolf. It rather appealed to him. As Alastair waited for him to catch up he charged with lowered head and bit him on the forearm. They tussled, giggles bursting from them like escaping gas.

'And soon or later we've got to stop being so greedy and wanting to hog everything for ever and ever or the world'll come to an end. There'll be nothing left but millions and millions of people, a large percentage of them very old and suffering, and nobody will have enough to eat or even enough space to lie down.'

They were all familiar with this dictum, and they all knew that it was true because Mr Bell said so.

'We found a cat that was run over but the vet didn't bother to make it better because it was too old.' Oliver escaped from Alastair and caught up with Mr Bell.

'Bad luck.'

'Its name was Elderberry.'

The excitement and novelty of the last few days had done a good healing job on Oliver's sensibilities and he was now able to talk of the cat without grief. In fact he was quite eager to talk to Mr Bell about it in a manly offhand sort of way.

'It was a very nice cat, but when we saw how old it was we said we'd better have it put to sleep.'

Mr Bell gave him a sharp glance and agreed that it had probably been the most sensible decision. 'But I expect you miss it, don't you?'

'Not while I'm here, I don't.'

It was true, for Oliver had already discovered that he adored the whole business of camping even more than he had thought possible. He tackled chores with relish, accepted discipline with equanimity, and exulted in living like all the famous explorers used to. They slept four to a tent, with Mr Bell occupying one all to himself, and they ate an enormous amount, finishing up with biscuits and sweets in the privacy of their sleeping bags long after official lights out. He couldn't get over the sweet pungent smell of newly trampled grass, and on the first night fell asleep in the middle of an argument with Alastair.

'I can hear the dew falling outside our tent.'

'No, you can't.'

'Yes, I can.'

'No you can't because dew doesn't fall downwards it comes upwards.'

'Huh. Who says?'

'Everybody who isn't a thick nit like you are...'

Silence. The other two occupants of the tent already asleep. Then outside the rustle of leaves and the shivering cry of a faraway owl.

'A few drops of it may come upwards,' Oliver admitted, rousing himself. 'But most of it comes downwards. Otherwise how do things that aren't on the ground get wet?'

'Condensation.'

'You don't get condensation out of doors, you fat nit.'

'Do.'

'Don't...'

Then waking early next morning and scrambling pyjama-clad out of the fuggy little tent to where the dew, wherever it had come from, lay sparkling on the grass like millions of tiny green-flecked diamonds.

The park in which they had permission to camp belonged to a large Palladian mansion with a lake in front of it and its own church snuggled close up to its left side. Rooks cawed in the flat-headed cedars, but they never saw any other sign of life. Alastair said that it was owned by a mad count who carried out experiments on people in the dungeons, while Oliver preferred the idea that it had been empty for centuries and was now littered with the dead people who had once owned it. They were all skeletons of course, but still dressed in all their old-fashioned clothes. Then Mr Bell put paid to their speculations by stating that it was owned by the local council, who used it for various welfare purposes. And that they happened to be one of them.

During the afternoon of their fourth day they set off for the lake with their swimming things, and Alastair had some flippers and a schnorkel which his American aunt had given him. He promised to let Oliver have a go. Away from the pressures of ordinary life their friendship seemed to have renewed itself, possibly encouraged by the fact that they didn't care for the other two boys in their tent. One wore a vest, and the other talked in his sleep.

The lake was quite shallow, with water lilies in the centre but no weeds. They changed in the privacy of some giant gunneras and were about to make a dash for the water when Mr Bell appeared.

'Fold your clothes up,' he said. 'Each lot in a separate pile with shoes at the bottom and towel on top.'

They stared at him for a moment before frisking back to do as they were told. Undressed, Mr Bell had the same pale and anonymous tidiness about him that he had in uniform. His skin above the forearms and below the narrow triangle at his neck was light pink and not very hairy. His black swimming trunks fitted neatly at the waist and his short fair hair was brushed down in its usual fashion. Even his expression of quiet watchfulness was exactly the same.

But then, with the sudden gasping elation of being in the water, everything seemed to change. Normal attitudes and conventions disappeared; there was no more sense of hierarchy and certainly no respect. Abruptly they made Mr Bell one of them, and kept seizing him in their wet sharp hands and trying to duck him, then trying to leap onto his back, their graceful little bodies agile and slippery, their laughter wild and ear-splittingly shrill.

They used him like a piece of sports equipment; they baited him as if he were a manageable yet potentially dangerous animal; they tried to blind him by beating on the surface of the water as if it were a drum, then did their best to obliterate him behind a frenzy of foam whipped up by their violently kicking legs. They attacked him, swam hastily away choking and spitting, then returned for another bout. They were like minnows, like fierce, laughing little mermen with their hair flattened over their streaming faces, and he played with them in return, grabbing them by the scruffs of their necks and dunking them rapidly, then lifting them high out of the water and throwing them back in again so that they disappeared, shrieking, in another cloud of spray. The water lilies rocked and bobbed with merriment, Alastair lost one of his flippers and an accidental blow on the cheek loosened one of Oliver's remaining milk teeth, but nothing mattered in the churning swirling battle in which nobody won and nobody lost.

Then as abruptly as it had started, it finished. Mr Bell stood up, and through a glittering sunshot rainbow Oliver saw him shake the water from his eyes and then remain motionless, staring at the shore. He saw him change back into the old familiar Mr Bell, and then somehow go on changing; his face became cold and sharp with a kind of rage that Oliver had never encountered before, in anyone, and automatically he turned his gaze in the same direction.

He discovered that they had all become the centre of admiring attention from the side of the lake. A few feet from the gunneras was a row of elderly people, white hair gleaming, bifocals glinting in the sunlight as they smiled and nodded and pointed with their walking sticks. Two of them were in wheelchairs. At first they seemed quite harmless, but something of Mr Bell's quiet and controlled hatred transferred itself to Oliver in the form of a strange fear. The old people became a threat; something ugly and unpleasant, and automatically he moved a little closer to Mr Bell and felt glad when the sides of their bare wet legs touched. But Mr Bell shifted slightly and the contact ceased.

'Out – everyone out now!'

The wild exuberance died. The others stopped their gambolling and made obediently for the shore, tired and panting. Noticing Oliver, Mr Bell placed his hand on top of his head and waded with him towards the onlookers.

The old people continued to nod and smile, exposing their plastic teeth.

'What's the water like? Nice and warm?'

'Just like the seaside, isn't it?'

'Wish we could join you...'

Benevolence flowed from them, but Oliver

began to shiver. The chattering of his teeth drew his attention to his loosened tooth and for a moment it seemed as if the sun had gone behind a cloud.

'Pick up your clothes,' Mr Bell ordered, and without acknowledging the friendliness of the spectators pushed a pathway through them and marched his group of Young Citizens back to camp in their wet swimming trunks.

The only person who spoke on the way was Alastair, who asked if he could go back and look for his flipper.

'Tomorrow.'

'Won't it sink deeper in the mud?'

'No.'

They were dry long before they reached the tents, and most of them flopped out in the shade, content to lie in a dreamy sleepy state without speaking. With his forearm shielding his eyes Oliver listened to the lazy squabbling of two sparrows, then heard someone ask who all those old men and women were.

'They're staying at the big house.'

'Why?'

'Somebody said they're all invalids and live in hospitals and they've come here as a treat.' He recognised the voice of the vest-wearer from his own tent. He knew a lot, and took it all very seriously.

'Be nice if it was somebody our age. We could go over and raid them.'

'That's not what we're here for,' Vest said primly. 'Mr Bell doesn't like violence.'

'He didn't mind a bit of it when we were in the lake.'

'That was different. It was only fooling about.'

'That's all we'd be doing, if...'

Oh shut up, thought Oliver, and tried to keep his tongue from probing his loose tooth. It was beginning to hurt.

Mrs Portman-Ayres' musical evening was not quite what Mrs Dansie had envisaged. In place of wobbling sopranos accompanied by decrepit amateur pianists, she found that the music was to be provided by record-player only, with Mrs Portman-Ayres in the role of disc-jockey.

She had arrived in good time, and was immediately interested to discover that Mrs Portman-Ayres also lived in a granny flat, in her case a portioned-off wing of the main family house. There was a lot of Capo di Monte and satin-stripe wallpaper, and the grand piano had on it a signed photograph of Dame Nellie Melba shrouded in sables. A gold tea-trolley, laden with coffee cups and little paper napkins, stood discreetly against the wall.

'My dear, how nice of you...'

Mrs Portman-Ayres shook her hand and touched her cheek with her own. 'Come and be introduced to Kitty and Winifred, two dear friends of mine and so musical–'

The two very old ladies sitting by the fireplace holding tiny glasses of sherry smiled at Mrs Dansie with faded eyes and touched her hand with fingers dry and delicate as tissue paper.

'How very pleasant, Mrs ah–'

'Dansie. Celia Dansie–'

'And how do you like living in the neighbourhood, Mrs–'

'I'm very happy here, thank you. Do you live–'

'Dr Bramford is our doctor. He was at school with the Archbishop of York–'

'Not the present one, Kitty.'

'I don't believe I've had the pleasure...' Mrs Dansie accepted her thimbleful of sherry with a bright smile.

'Dr Bramford nursed our poor brother to the very end. Dear Rufus, we still can't quite take it in–'

'I'm so very sorry to hear–'

'Seventeen years in Singapore. The climate took its toll.'

'How very sad–'

'Have you any family, Mrs ah–'

Without waiting for her to reply they were off on another subject, skipping from one to another like two little bees among the hollyhocks.

Mrs Dansie's rescue was effected by a

large bald man who took her hand in a large warm paw and said: 'How nice to see a bit of new blood.'

It was difficult to think of a reply that was neither chill nor coquettish, so she smiled and said nothing.

'The wife was coming as well, then decided she'd got one of her migraine-things. Congenitally nervous woman, I'm afraid.'

Again it was difficult to find a suitable reply. Murmuring something conventionally sympathetic Mrs Dansie looked round in the vain hope that she might see someone she knew. The room had about two dozen people in it now, and she found herself gazing at Mrs Portman-Ayres' little coterie of retired music-lovers; silver-haired ladies clutching little evening bags, stertorous old gentlemen with whiskers in their ears, and she didn't know one of them. She began to feel almost physically ill with the longing for Bertie. If only Bertie had been standing by her side, tall and rather stooping after years of bending over a dentist's chair, and quietly cupping her elbow in his hand and giving it a little squeeze every now and then...

Her reverie was interrupted by Mrs Portman-Ayres clapping her hands together and suggesting that the recital should begin. Everyone found a seat, and Mrs Dansie shared a small settee with a vivacious old lady wearing a little piece of jewelled netting on her head.

'You're Mrs Campbell, aren't you?'

'No, my name is Dansie. Celia Dansie.'

'But I expect you *know* Mrs Campbell, don't you?'

'I'm afraid not.'

'Didn't we meet at Mrs Dennington's coffee morning?'

'I don't think so.'

'Well, I'm giving one in aid of the cancer scanner next Friday week. *Do* say you'll be able to come…'

Whether by accident or design they were all now sitting in two rows facing the grand piano and a single rose-coloured *fauteuil*. The record-player, a daunting affair with all its mechanism on view inside a transparent box, was against the wall nearest the piano. In total silence Mrs Portman-Ayres approached it and raised the lid.

'I thought we would begin with something light-hearted,' she said, and taking the record from its cover, held it poised in butterfly fingers above the turntable. 'The Brahms A Minor Quartet, published in 1873 and dedicated to his dear old friend Theodor Billroth.'

To the sound of small sighs and flutterings of expectancy she set the record playing and then moved to the lone *fauteuil*, where she seated herself with due care and attention to detail. The one light left on in the room fell upon her, illuminating her dress and her statuesque pose while leaving everyone else in rather dreary summer twilight.

The music began, and within three minutes of weaving its gracious airy little garlands the audience appeared to have fallen into some kind of trance, eyes closed, expressions (so far as could be seen) rapt. A little fearfully Mrs Dansie peered round at them all, but found her attention riveted to her hostess. She too was sitting with eyes closed, one shapely hand supporting her chin, and the soft glow of lamplight caressed a face that was totally without wrinkles or blemishes.

My God, she's had it lifted! thought Mrs Dansie, and the music paused in its weaving and gave a little high shriek.

Feeling like the only schoolgirl left awake in the dorm she closed her eyes like the rest of them and tried resolutely to concentrate on the music, but it was beginning to get on her nerves. Dodging and dancing about, it made her think of a blowfly in pursuit of a mosquito. And mosquitoes made her think of the tropics, which made her think of poor Rufus in Singapore, and then of the two little Ugandans whom Willow and Seth had planned to adopt. The plan had now fallen through apparently, and no one seemed to speak of it any more.

After the Brahms they had a Beethoven String Trio, Mrs Portman-Ayres rousing herself with slow elegant movements and gliding towards the record-player like a sleepwalker. During the most poignant moments of Schubert's Death and the Maiden Quartet Mrs Dansie was stricken with cramp in her left calf. Pressing her foot hard on the floor and gritting her teeth in agony she thought Stand up, you fool. Rub your leg, walk round the room – they'll never notice if you stand on your head.

But of course she remained where she was. With beads of perspiration on her forehead she watched her companion's jewelled old fingers twiddling rapturously at an imaginary violin and knew that she would sooner suffer slow death than risk interrupting the sublimity all around her.

They awoke slowly, some moments after the final chords had faded, then gratefully applauded Mrs Portman-Ayres while Mrs Dansie stood up and rubbed discreetly at her simmering calf muscles.

'Gramophones have changed a great deal recently,' confided the old lady with whom she had shared the settee. 'The dear old one we had at home had to be wound by hand.'

A woman in a print smock sidled into the room with a large coffee pot. She returned with some sandwiches, then propelled the gold trolley reverently towards Mrs Portman-Ayres' *fauteuil* before sidling out again.

Conversation became animated, and they were all sipping and nibbling when the large bald man suddenly said that he hoped no one was thinking of going on an old people's coach trip this summer. His voice carried across the room, drowning the tinkle of teaspoons.

'I can't imagine that anyone here...' Mrs Portman-Ayres left the rest of the sentence hanging delicately in mid-air.

'Why do you hope they aren't?' asked Mrs Dansie, interested.

'It was in the news this evening that there's been another accident. A coachload of over-sixties skidded off the road, crashed through a fence and rolled down an embankment. Four killed and seventeen injured.'

There were shocked exclamations, which he interrupted. 'This makes the fourth accident of its kind this summer.'

'They drive too fast,' cried an old gentleman in surgical boots. 'The roads are too crowded and everyone drives too *fast*–'

'That's not the point, Commander,' the bald man said. 'The point is that all these coach accidents have happened to elderly people. To people of our age group.'

There was a momentary silence. Mrs Portman-Ayres removed a tiny shred of watercress from her upper lip.

'It must be a coincidence, Stanley,' she said finally. 'Statistically speaking there must be more ah – coachloads of retired people on the roads than any other sort, so if there have to be coach accidents at all, it follows that the elderly are likely to suffer more heavily.'

'What about children?' someone said from the other side of the room. 'Hundreds get taken to school in coaches every day, and nothing ever happens to them.'

Commander – Stanley, thought Mrs Dansie. I'm in a world of strangers. I've as much in common with these people as I have with Batman or the Archers...

'Children have far too much these days,' a reedy little voice piped from behind a cucumber sandwich. 'When we were young we had to walk.'

'It did us good–'

'We were far better for it–'

'Are you suggesting that the elderly are being singled out for some kind of retributive punishment?' Mrs Dansie hadn't meant to speak so loudly. The crisp clarity of her voice made her blush slightly.

'Why not?' The bald man called Stanley turned to look at her. 'Hitler persecuted the Jews, didn't he?'

'What's that got to do with it?' She stared back at him. And then suddenly remembered saying something equally fatuous to Seth about the Hitler Youth Movement.

'It's probably got nothing to do with it. I mentioned it merely as an example of human ingenuity when it comes to inventing excuses for hatred.'

'But Stanley dear,' Mrs Portman-Ayres said indulgently, 'why should anyone hate us? Of all sectors of the general public surely we elderly are the least likely to be victimised. Few of us go to football matches, lurk about the streets after dark, smoke pot, carry knives or have extreme political convictions–'

'On the other hand, you could regard our age group as a kind of corporate sitting duck,' Stanley said. 'We're a pretty safe target for any fanatical nut who wants to vent his spleen on society in general because we're no longer vigorous enough to protect ourselves. I may look a hale and hearty bloke but it's only due to a pacemaker. Without it I'd have conked out three years ago.'

'All bullies are cowards,' someone said knowledgeably.'

'Yes, but why–' began Mrs Dansie. '*Why* should–'

'For our next little recital I was toying with the idea of Monterverdi,' Mrs Portman-Ayres said with sudden smooth authority. 'In fact I thought it might be rather fun to consider his development of the *aria* and its influence on the work of Scarlatti.' It was obvious that the subject of possible sabotage of the elderly bored her.

'Oh Beatrice, how splendid!' The old lady who had shared Mrs Dansie's settee clasped her hands in rapture. 'Could we include Orfeo?'

'Of course we could, Dolly dear. All we need is to fix a date suitable to us all.'

There was a hasty fumbling for pocket diaries. Across the flutter of tiny pages Mrs Dansie caught the eye of the man Stanley, who hunched his shoulders resignedly.

It took a long while for the date to be fixed, but the vigorous discussion that ensued diverted everyone's mind from the unpleasantness of the previous subject and the evening ended on a tranquil note. At the door of Mrs Portman-Ayres' granny flat Stanley put his hand on Mrs Dansie's shoulder and asked if he could give her a lift home.

'It's very kind of you, but I have my own car.'

'Oh.' He looked disappointed, then grinned at her. 'Well, you can't blame me for trying.'

They walked out into the drive together.

'Do you really think there's some sort of underground movement pledged to getting rid of elderly people?' She tried to sound casual, amused.

'Yes, I do.' They paused by her car. 'Something must explain all these deaths by misadventure that you read of in the papers. Brakes don't fail on coaches without a good reason any more than old ladies fall under buses without being pushed.'

Her heartbeat quickened slightly. For a

moment she was tempted to tell him of Oliver's strange little hints about the dangers of proclaiming her age to all and sundry; she realised that she had been longing to talk to someone about that weirdly constrained last-but-one visit of his to the granny flat, yet she allowed the moment to pass. She didn't know the man well enough, and didn't like him sufficiently to entrust him with a confidence. So she bade him goodnight and got into the car.

'We ought to discuss this thing in more detail,' he said. 'Perhaps I could meet you for a drink one evening?'

'Perhaps you should discuss it with your wife first,' Mrs Dansie suggested gently, smiled and drove away.

Lights were on in the main house when she reached home and she could hear the sounds of laughter. She would have liked to call in, but the three strange cars in the courtyard deterred her. She didn't belong there any more than she belonged to Mrs Portman-Ayres' lot.

Parking in her allotted space in the garage she went up to her own quarters, bolting the door behind her.

'Oliver's cat is a very good example of what we're talking about,' Amory Bell said.

Sitting on a straw bale, he bent forward to throw another lump of wood onto the fire.

Sparks flew up, illuminating the ring of impressionable young faces and the pale glimmer of tents in the background.

'We think it's kind to put an old sick animal to sleep, but we're afraid to perform the same merciful act for a human being. Hands up those who think it's unfair.'

All hands went up, as he knew they would. And he knew with equal certainty those that were raised in genuine conviction and those in mere politeness. Each year was the same, with the little boys in his group already privately assessed in terms of promising or non-promising material long before the summer holidays came. And then with the advent of camp with all its unique charm, its strange primeval whisperings mingled with the jolly flavour of masculine compatibility, it was merely a question of confirming his initial assessment and of getting quietly to work on the promising material while discarding, without any tangible sign of doing so, the type of little boy who was born prosaic, pigheaded and thus incorruptible. He loved them all with a curious tenderness quite devoid of sensualism, seeking in each polished upturned face the hungry, hesitant shadow of the Amory Bell whose parents had abandoned him to the grasp of an old, rotting grandmother. For the past eight years his life had been silently dedicated to the prevention of such grotesque and terrible relationships ever being formed anywhere again.

The flames of the campfire leaped higher, licking the heavens and dancing on the circle of bobbed hair, shining eyes, freckled noses and mouths crammed with spearmint, bubblegum and gobstoppers. Yes, he loved them all, and knew that he had the ability to mark some of them for life with the power of his convictions; the boy Alastair was a possibility, and perhaps something could be done with the red-headed one they called Chuffer, but when his gaze came finally to rest on the eager, exultant little face of Oliver Mitchell he knew that this year he was planning to expend all his skill on the processing of one single pupil of unusual promise and outstanding necessity.

The decision had in fact been taken almost three months ago, on the evening Oliver had made the grave error of inviting his grandmother to the Young Citizens' concert.

'Can we have a game, Mr Bell?'

The high treble voice came from somewhere in the circle, jolting him out of his reverie.

'What sort of game, Rob?'

'Murder.'

'Ah yes, let's play *Murder!*'

'Ah c'mon, let's play *Murder – can't* we, Mr Bell?–'

The circle was broken now and they clustered round him, jostling and jiggling

172

with impatience.

Normally he liked the day to end on a quiet, thoughtful note, but tonight they were still too full of energy to sleep, and anyway – he permitted himself the ghost of a smile – to play *Murder* was not all that inappropriate.

'Okay – you've got half an hour before bed and lights out so you'd better look sharp.'

He organised them swiftly and competently, pulling a handful of straws from one of the bales and arranging them so that they could draw lots.

'One straw's still got an ear of corn, and whoever gets that is the murderer and he mustn't let on to anyone else. Another straw's got a knot in it, and whoever gets that one is the detective. Right now, who's got detective?'

A hand went up.

'Okay. You stay here with me until the murder's been committed. The rest of you get together in twos and try to find somewhere where you think you'll be safe, but don't forget – we don't know who the murderer is. It might be your partner, so keep your eye on him. Right – off you go.'

They scattered, dodging nimbly in and out of the shadows. The fire was dying down but the moon was rising like a pale apricot over the trees and he was aware of perfect contentment. Camp had gone well this summer, and his careful drip-feed teaching would even now be trickling along the dark little conduits of their minds and preparing the timid-sheep majority to accept the idea of mercy killing when they were older. As for the others, each year had so far produced at least one likely candidate for eventual admission into the ultra-secret group of Young Fighting Citizens, whose highly specialised activities were of vital importance until self-destruction at the age of sixty became compulsory. Then, and only then, would their work become obsolete.

Officially of course, the Young Fighting Citizens didn't exist; there was nothing in writing, no special emblems were worn and no slogans were chanted. But they had become attached, like some mysterious growth invisible to the naked eye, onto the main stem of the healthy, hearty Young Citizens, and like most forms of parasitic life were able to multiply with rapidity. Amory Bell was sole instigator, but even he was unable to say with accuracy how many belonged to the elite band of young exterminators. The realisation brought him great satisfaction.

'I got detective, what do I have to do now?' It was the vest-wearing boy who sidled round the bonfire towards him.

'You don't have to do anything until someone's been murdered, Paul. Then it's your job to find out who did it.'

The boy hung about uncertainly, the glow from the fire emphasising his bare legs and short socks. All the others wore jeans.

Amory indicated a vacant patch on the straw bale beside him and after a moment's hesitation the boy seated himself. They listened in silence to the scufflings and snapping of twigs in the distance. Shadows flitted between the trees, and when a small wavering cry rose on the still air it was impossible to tell whether it was a bird or a boy. The night seemed to throb with strange and mysterious elements.

'I think it's wrong to kill people, Mr Bell.'

'It's only a game.'

'I mean, what you said tonight about old people.'

'Oh, that.' Naturally he had encountered this reaction in previous years, so there was no difficulty in feigning indifference. 'You don't have to take everything too seriously, you know.'

'But I think old people are *nice*.'

'We all do, Paul. Which is one of the reasons why responsible people worry about them. We don't want them to feel pain and loneliness, and it's because of this very concern that some of us – a handful of special, intelligent people like you and me and the other boys here – like to talk over the problem of how we can save old people from suffering.'

'My grandad's eighty-five and he doesn't suffer–'

'How d'you know? Have you ever asked him?' For a moment his voice was sharp. Too sharp.

'Well, no. But...'

'There you are. And of course no one in his right mind barges up to old folk and says Excuse me, are you suffering? If he did, the chances are he'd get his ear clipped.'

The boy gave a reluctant little cackle.

'No, no, Paul, don't get the wrong end of the stick. We're not trying to teach you that all old people should be put to sleep like – well, like Oliver Mitchell's cat. We were only talking about the sadness of old people being ill and unhappy and being forced to go on living in houses and eating food which could be put to better purpose by young people like you, and all because doctors won't let them die when they want to. But it's nothing to get in a sweat about. We were only talking in a general sort of way, man to man round the campfire.'

He turned to look at the boy beside him. His square, rather lugubrious young face had a troubled, almost tearful look in the moonlight.

'Well, none of us would let my granddad suffer.'

'Of course you wouldn't,' Amory agreed. 'And that's all that matters, isn't it?'

He would have to go carefully with young Paul. But like the handful of other little boys who, over the past eight years, had challenged his careful indoctrination, Paul's non-conformity was based on timidity and lack of imagination. Although good at learning he was not a bright boy, and if he should tell his parents that Mr Bell had said that all old people should be put to sleep, no one would believe a child of nine or ten in preference to an experienced youth leader.

It had already happened twice before, and on each occasion it had been simplicity itself to deny all knowledge of such a preposterous idea. If necessary he was quite capable of denying it in the face of his entire group of Young Citizens plus their parents and plus the official administration of the Council of Young Citizens, although he knew that such a situation was unlikely to arise. Little boys loved gangs and secrets far too much, and if the ultimate should ever happen he was quite prepared to die for the cause he believed in.

In any case, he would die for it on the day he was sixty.

A piercing scream rang out from the darkness of the trees. It faded on a deep gurgling note and Amory felt the boy sitting next to him start convulsively.

'I don't like playing this.'

'We can't very well tell the others that or they'll call you chicken. Come on, someone's done the murder, and now it's up to you to find out who it was. This is the best part of the game.'

They waited side by side while small shadowy figures materialised through the gloom. Amory threw some more wood on the fire and a plume of white smoke arose.

'Well, who's been deaded?'

'Martin has.'

'It's Martin.'

'Martin's lying over there by the bushes – his throat's been cut with a knife.'

'No, it hasn't, he's been strangled by a maniac.'

'His heart's been torn out.'

'He's not by the bushes, he's nearer the latrines–'

They were hopping and jumping like taut little coils of wire.

'All right, all right, simmer down. And remember that whichever of you's the murderer, he's got to try and sling the crime on to someone else. So when the detective questions you, tell the truth about where you were when the crime was committed unless you want to be falsely accused. Right, Paul, off you go.'

Sitting cross-legged on the straw bale Amory gave an encouraging shove to the boy Paul, who wriggled and then tried despairingly to adopt a detective-like pose.

'Now then, all you lot, who's been killed?'

'Martin has.'

'It's *Martin.*'

'I think you'll have to go and inspect the corpse for yourself,' Amory murmured.

Unwillingly Paul went towards the dark belt of trees followed by the others, all of them pushing and shoving and chattering excitedly. The corpse lay spreadeagled dramatically.

'Is he really dead?'

'Of course he is, you feeble nit.'

'Well, who did it? Come on, own up.'

They returned to where Amory sat prodding at the fire with a long stick. The white plume of smoke dispersed in a sudden burst of flame. Sparks flew heavenward and they were all illuminated in a lurid orange light.

'Martin's the corpse,' Paul said wretchedly. 'What shall I do now, Mr Bell?'

'Start questioning them. Find out by trial and error who's responsible.'

Poor young Paul with the silly shorts and woolly vest, he didn't want to play a game for which he had no natural aptitude. And the little monsters sensed his reluctance, his awkward, worried attempts to ask sensible questions in a stupid feigned voice. They pranced round him in the leaping firelight, mocking him, imitating him, and it was obvious that they were hellbent on physical action and had no time for the tedious business of solving Martin's murder.

With a face devoid of expression Amory let them go their own way, and watched them wrestling, tussling, and exploding with mirth. Night was the time for madness, for the shedding of inhibitions, and Martin grew tired of being a corpse and came over to join them.

And strangely enough, the boy at the heart of it all was Oliver Mitchell. He had never been like this before. Whooping and shrieking he pranced in and out of the crowd, flapping his hands and grimacing hideously. They couldn't help laughing at him. Someone tripped him up and he fell with a quavering cry, tried to raise himself on palsied limbs and then fell down again. He writhed and fluttered, and when they hauled him up and set him on his feet he spun round in crazy little circles, quivering and quavering and dribbling in a frenzied study of senility, a condition he had never even seen. And the others, recognising the character, seized him with a gleeful shout and dragged him towards the fire.

What shall we do with the dirt and the dregs?
We'll tidy it up – we'll tidy it up!...

They were back in the concert, and they swung him by the arms and legs, higher and higher, so that the moon rushed into the orange flames and then flew clear again. All the world was black and gold and wild and beautiful and nobody wanted it to end; not even Paul, who together with Alastair, was now helping to swing Oliver by the neck of his tee-shirt.

We'll tidy it up – we'll–

'Okay, that's enough. Save some for tomorrow.'

Perhaps in their exultation they would have actually flung Oliver into the fire if Amory hadn't called them to order. But at the quiet sound of his voice the lust for action died. They were no longer a pack. They dropped Oliver back on his feet and he went giddily across to Mr Bell, tucking his tee-shirt back in his jeans.

'Can I be the tramp next time, Mr Bell? Next time we have the concert can I be the tramp instead of–'

'We'll have to see.'

And the most surprising part of that surprising climax to the evening was Mr Bell's facial expression. Normally pale and blank, and with feelings brushed tidily aside in the way that he brushed his hair, it was now warm and glowing, and the smile pressing out the corners of his mouth was reflected in his eyes.

'But in the meantime everyone's going to get cracking clearing up the mess they've made. I can see at least ten toffee papers even from here. And then it's heads down and lights out in ten minutes sharp.'

They scurried obediently. The moon changed from apricot to pure hard silver, and Oliver fell asleep magnificent in the knowledge that he was capable of playing any part in any concert that Mr Bell might be planning for the future.

'Yes, I think it's very nice dear, but isn't it a bit cramped, after–'

'After Chantry Lodge, you mean? But I wouldn't want all that space now, would I?'

'It would depend on what you're thinking of doing.'

'I'm not thinking of doing anything, Bella.'

Smiling, but with hackles slightly raised, the two sisters stood regarding one another. Mrs Dansie in a blue cotton dress and a string of red beads, and Mrs Frewin in a pale green drip-dry. She had just arrived from Denbighshire for a ten-day visit.

'No, of course not,' she said, with the air of someone who had given up expecting anything years ago. 'I was forgetting you're sixty.'

'Seeing that an invitation to the party is the express reason for your being here, I find that difficult to believe.'

'Now then, Celia, don't start getting prickly. Go and pour us a drink, there's a good girl.'

Mrs Dansie went. She felt extraordinarily pleased and relieved to see Bella, and it occurred to her for the first time that they probably bickered because they enjoyed it.

'You're thinner,' Mrs Frewin said, sipping gin and dry ginger. 'Has Willow got you up to your eyes in nappy-washing and pram-pushing?'

'Quite the opposite. She makes a point of running a baby with the same competence with which she runs her job.'

'See much of her?'

'No. But we've got it all worked out.'

'It's fatal to become too involved in one's children's lives.'

'I couldn't agree more,' Mrs Dansie said with a touch of fervour. 'As it is, our relationship is based on mutual respect and the knowledge that we can always call on one another in times of trouble.'

'Sounds ideal. How's Oliver?'

'Away at camp with the Young Citizens. Having a wonderful time, I believe.'

'You know, I always visualised you all going off to the seaside together, somehow. Mummy and Daddy, the children and dear old Granny all playing games on the beach and then Granny going off for a decorous little paddle–'

'Seth and Willow have got too much work on to take a holiday this year. After all, they're just starting to build up the practice and as

Willow says, Humphrey is really too young to appreciate going away. But next year–'

'Funny, I've never been keen on the idea of Scouts and camping and all that for little boys–'

'This *isn't* the Scouts, Bella. It's something entirely different.'

'I don't care what it calls itself – it's all the same idea. Little impressionable boys at the mercy of some weird chap in khaki shorts–'

'You're talking nonsense.' A little nerve began to jump in Mrs Dansie's cheek. She took a sip from her glass.

'Celia, dear, I don't care what you say but any grown man who wants to spend his summer holidays living in a tent with a lot of little boys *is* weird. He's either worryingly creepy or dreadfully immature–'

'Oh dry up!' cried Mrs Dansie with sudden violence. 'Stop being so bloody knowledge-able–'

'Me? Knowledgeable? I only wish I were.'

'The trouble is that everything in Den-bighshire's thirty years behind the times and whenever you come down here you think that everything we've got that you haven't must obviously be all wrong.'

'Don't be childish.'

'I'm not. I was merely–' Mrs Dansie pressed her lips tightly together and drew a deep breath. She *was* being childish, but then so was Bella. In silence she took their empty glasses over to the drinks table and refilled them.

'Cheers.'

'Cheers.'

They sipped, eyes averted from one another.

'Harold was very pleased with Bertie's golf clubs, by the way. He's taking lessons.'

'Oh, good.'

'Celia–' Mrs Frewin suddenly leaned forward in her chair, scrutinizing her sister '–you are all right, aren't you? I mean, you are happy here, and everything?'

'Yes, of course I am. Why?'

'I don't know. I just had a funny feeling running down my back–'

'I'll close the window,' Mrs Dansie said abruptly. 'You're sitting in a draught.'

On the night before camp ended Oliver's loose tooth started hurting. Really hurting, as opposed to the spasmodic twinge when he bit on it.

Lying in the darkness of the tent he tried to keep his tongue away from it but it kept wandering back of its own volition, probing and poking and making it worse. He turned restlessly resentful that he was the only one awake. The dim hump of Alastair lay close and he gave it a sudden wallop with his arm. Alastair stirred.

'What's the difference between a seagull

and a baby?'

Alastair sighed without waking.

'Listen, what's the difference between a seagull and a baby? Come on, it's a rude one.'

'Shuddup.'

'All right, fat nit, I won't tell you.'

Oliver flung himself over on his face and his tooth gave a fierce leap. He sat up, rocking to and fro.

'I've got toothache. It's hurting.'

No one answered. No one cared. And mingling with the pain of his tooth was the desolation of knowing that camp was at an end. Tomorrow they would all be going home. He couldn't bear the idea. He wanted to go on living in the tent with Alastair and the others even when it was winter.

But most of all, he wanted to go on living with Mr Bell. He had always had a strange, special feeling for him, and on the night they had played *Murder* the feeling had crystallised into something deeper. It was because of Mr Bell that he had been able to clown and make everyone laugh. With Mr Bell close at hand he could do anything; be clever, be funny, be brave, and to return to the old routine of seeing him only once a week was becoming more and more unendurable. His tooth gave another lurch.

Holding his jaw with one hand Oliver scrambled out of his sleeping bag and stumbled outside. The moon had gone but the stars were very bright. He picked his way over to Mr Bell's small tent, and the sound of a quiet voice made him start.

'Yes, Oliver? What is it?'

Mr Bell was sitting in the opening of his tent as if he had been waiting for him. Oliver could see the smooth outline of his head against the canvas.

'My tooth hurts.' But the surprise of finding Mr Bell awake and composed in the middle of the night was so great that the pain ceased.

'Is it a loose tooth? Come here.'

Mr Bell reached behind him into the dark recess of the tent and a beam of torchlight illuminated Oliver's bare feet and rumpled pyjamas.

'I don't want it pulled out–'

'Kneel down and let's have a look.'

Oliver knelt, and opening his mouth pointed inside.

'That one?'

'Yes, but don't–'

'It's only handing by a thread.'

'Yes, but I don't want–'

'Shall I pull it out?'

Mr Bell's face was in shadow behind the torchlight. Dazzled, Oliver could only see a silhouette outlined in a soft golden haze, but his nearness was so powerful that it was like being with God or someone. Once more he had the feeling that he could do anything, be anything, because of Mr Bell.

'Shall I pull it out?' Mr Bell's hand was resting on top of Oliver's head, tilting it backwards. Oliver swallowed hard.

'Yes.'

'We often have to do things we don't want to. Things that are going to hurt a bit. So we just have to concentrate on the fact that we know that what we're doing is right.'

'Yes.'

'Something we'll never be ashamed of.'

'Yes.'

'Tell you what, why don't *you* pull it out?'

'Me?'

Only that minute resigned to the idea that Mr Bell should do it, Oliver floundered and all but fell to pieces. The palms of his hands became hot.

'I can't.'

'Why not?'

'I – I don't know exactly where it is.' The glare of the torch made black circles dance in front of his eyes.

'Yes you do. Go on.'

The hand on top of Oliver's head was firm and kind and very cool. His own were now sticky with sweat.

'I know you're a brave boy, Oliver. And if you can do this, I'll rate you as someone very special. Very special indeed.'

'Will you give me a present?' Oliver regretted the craven words immediately.

They made him sound a horrible baby nit.

'Not a present exactly,' Mr Bell said. 'But I'll give you the chance to do something very special, and very very brave.'

'Will it hurt more than this?'

'No. It'll just hurt in a different sort of way.'

'What is it?'

'Pull your tooth out first.'

Two sweaty fingers crept reluctantly towards his lower lip. They touched the tooth and slid away.

'Go on. Get it over with.'

Oliver closed his eyes. The black circles disappeared but he could still see the golden halo outlining Mr Bell's head. Perhaps he *was* God. Taking a deep breath and screwing up his face he made a lightning grab at the tooth, missed it, grabbed again and felt the quick taste of salty blood.

'Good boy. I'm proud of you.'

'It didn't hurt. I didn't feel anything at all.'

'Here.' Mr Bell removed his hand from the top of Oliver's head and reached behind him into the tent again. 'Have a peppermint. It'll make your mouth feel nicer.'

Normally Oliver didn't like peppermints, but on this occasion the taste was just right. Clean, antiseptic and very manly. He was glad that Mr Bell took one too.

'What shall I do with my tooth – chuck it away?' At home he always got fifty pence for a tooth, but home was unimaginably remote to him now.

Surprisingly, Mr Bell held out his hand. 'No, I'll keep it.'

'What for?'

'As a token of friendship, if you like.'

Oliver gave it to him and their fingers touched. They sat looking across the dim white circle of ash where the fire had been. The other tents glimmered on the far side of it. The starlight seemed very peaceful after the hot glare of the torch.

'I don't want to leave here,' Oliver said eventually.

'No?'

'I'd like to live here always.'

'Why?' Mr Bell's voice was very quiet.

'Because it's – well, because we all like doing the same things, and because it's fun.'

'And it's fun because there are no old people to spoil it.'

'No...' As if from a long way off Oliver remembered the time shortly before coming to camp when he had tried to inveigle Mr Bell into denying or confirming Alastair's tale about killing people when they got old and referring to it as Big Goodnight. He remembered, wonderingly, that the idea had upset him and made him dream at night.

'Do you remember all those old people down by the lake that day? Do you remember the way they all looked at us?'

Oliver sat trying to remember. And trying to keep his tongue out of the jellied little hole where his tooth had been.

'They looked at us with loathing.'

'Did they?' Even if they had, it didn't seem to matter now that he was here with Mr Bell. On the other hand it seemed to matter a lot to Mr Bell, and Mr Bell was always right about everything. Even about the things it was right to worry about. 'Yes, they did, didn't they?'

'But whatever they're like and however they treat us, we've got to remember to feel sorry for them. They're old and suffering and they shouldn't be kept alive.'

'No.'

Oliver finished his peppermint and wished he could ask for another one.

'But it takes very brave and very special people to help solve the problem. Want another peppermint?'

It was becoming increasingly clear that Mr Bell really was God because of the way he could read people's minds. Or if he wasn't actually God he was some other equally amazing kind of spaceman. Loving admiration made Oliver wriggle a little nearer and their knees touched. But Mr Bell shifted, and they parted again.

'What d'you want me to do that's very brave and special?'

'I want you to put someone to sleep.' Mr

191

Bell's voice seemed to be coming from inside Oliver's head. 'Someone who's old and pathetic and lives quite close to you.'

He knew whom he meant. And he didn't feel frightened or horrified. Sitting there in the warm starlight with Mr Bell he was aware only of the release of hidden tensions coupled with a sober and very adult sense of responsibility.

A hedgehog rustled under the trees looking for mice, while Oliver collected the words for the most vital question of all.

'If I told anyone about it, would they kill me?'

'No,' Mr Bell said very quietly and gently. 'They would kill me instead.'

'Oliver will be home tomorrow,' Willow said. 'I expect he's dying to be back.'

'Every young animal has an instinct for its nest.'

'I like to think of our home as a basic sort of nest. It may be old-fashioned, but what's wrong with that?'

She looked round the handsome kitchen, and at Seth, who was sitting with a sketch-pad on his knee. Humphrey was in bed, supper was over and the only sound to intrude on the loving silence was the distant gurgle of the dishwasher.

'I think it's time we had another baby.'

'Could you really cope, with the practice

and everything?' A row of smart little flat-roofed houses was appearing from under Seth's pencil.

'No problem. Anyway, as things are going we could probably afford an au pair. Although on second thoughts I'd rather have someone to do the rough so that I could supervise the children myself.'

'It was tough luck about the little Ugandans.'

'It honestly makes your blood boil, all that red tape and officialdom when it's human lives at stake.'

They sat thinking about them; picturing with sorrow the pot-bellies and little stick limbs, the rickets and ringworm that could all be put right so easily if only people would persevere more.

'I think Granny's been missing Oliver.'

'I know, she adores him. But at least she's got Auntie Bella now, hasn't she?'

'How long's she staying?'

'Until after the party. I've always liked Auntie Bella but I could never stand her daughter. Dear Betsy and I were supposed to have such a lot in common when we were children and no one ever seemed to notice how much we loathed one another.'

'I know,' said Seth, adding windows and doors. 'It's strange how few people seem to notice what goes with their own children.'

'I really must start planning the party

soon. I'm not even sure who's coming yet.'

'Has Granny made many local friends?'

'I'm not sure.' Willow frowned. 'Sometimes I don't think she really tries. Still, I suppose you don't have the same impetus when you're old.'

Reaching out a long thin arm she twiddled a tendril of ivy over the antique kitchen scales. Seth scribbled some foliage behind the flat-roofed houses.

'In fact, I'm not sure she's all that keen on having a party. She seems a bit hesitant, somehow.'

'Probably worried about the expense, bless her. Which reminds me, will she expect champagne or would some kind of ordinary sparkling wine do?'

'No use asking me,' Willow said. 'I always drink mineral water at parties.'

'Oliver's back tomorrow, isn't he?' Mrs Frewin said. 'I expect you'll be glad.'

'Yes. I will.'

'I haven't seen him since he was Humphrey's age.'

'You'll notice quite a change.'

'Betsy doesn't want to start a family for five years. I can see her point of course, but it must be nice having grandchildren. Particularly when they get to Oliver's age.'

'Yes,' said Mrs Dansie. 'You'll enjoy it very much.'

She spoke with sincerity, yet even her own ears caught the note of dubiety in her voice. She had now given up all hope of receiving a postcard from him, and the knowledge that his parents had received three had done nothing to diminish her anxiety. On the contrary, it had merely made her feel jealous.

Many times during the past two weeks she had brooded over the change in him, searching for reasons why his manner towards her should have become so markedly different. She tried to recall ticking him off, or being unfairly sharp with him, but couldn't. Apart from the episode of the cat, her most insistent memory was of the day he came up to her flat, nervous and constrained and stammering out that strange warning about not telling people that she was about to become sixty.

Something very bad and horrible could happen, so you mustn't go on telling all sorts of people outside, he had said, and the memory of his words always led her back to the conversation at Mrs Portman-Ayres' musical evening and to the man called Stanley who had a theory that elderly people had become a target for organised violence.

She didn't believe it. But neither could she forget it, and found herself searching the daily paper with increased attention for tucked away paragraphs about old folks and fatal accidents. She wished now that she hadn't been so prim with Stanley.

Twice she made up her mind to talk to Willow and Seth about it and then changed her mind, afraid of sounding ridiculous. Instead, she vowed to tell her sister as soon as a suitable opportunity arose; but with only the two of them in the granny flat suitable opportunities were occurring all the time, yet she said nothing. Bella was a dear, but not exactly renowned for understanding irrational fears. And the fears were irrational. Of course they were.

'Are you having your hair done for the party, Celia?'

'Oh – I expect so.'

'Then I'll come with you. After all, it's up to all the old girls to look their best, isn't it?'

'Old? Who's old?'

'You're going to be, dear. In another three days' time.'

When he arrived home, the sense of anti-climax was even worse than Oliver had envisaged. It all seemed so feeble and humdrum, so pointless and uninspiring. A house was a stupid place to live in compared to a tent, and when he told his parents so they smiled indulgently and said that a tent wouldn't be much fun in the winter.

'It would – it would! Some of them have proper floors and everything, and if you wear lots of clothes you never feel cold!'

Tears rushed to his eyes and he pushed his spinach soup away.

'Aren't you hungry, darling?'

'No.'

'Well, perhaps it might be a good idea to have a nice hot bath and then pop off to bed early. You can read until nine o'clock.'

'Okay.'

He trailed upstairs, wiping his nose on the back of his hand.

Nothing was any good any more. The only good thing had been Elderberry, but he had had to die because he was old and ill. The empty space down by the Aga renewed Oliver's grief and he realised that Elderberry had been far more than just a cat; he had been a kind and understanding friend and his loss was irreparable.

He looked round his bedroom at the model aeroplanes, the train layout, the box of Lego and the pile of tattered comics, and none of them meant anything. He remembered that he had hidden a Mars bar in his underwear drawer for when he returned, but made no attempt to unearth it. He just stood there thinking how stupid everything was.

Very slowly he went over to the bed and began to unzip the bright green waterproof pack that contained all his camping things. He tipped them out. Knife, spoon and fork. Sponge bag, torch, plastic mug, plastic food box and a pile of dirty clothes. Biscuit crumbs fell out of his sleeping bag and his swimming trunks were still damp. He took the clothes up in a bunch and carried them along to the bathroom. They smelt of wood-smoke and baked beans, chewing gum and wet grass and hot sunshine, and he dropped them one by one into the dirty linen basket knowing that they would never be the same after they had been washed.

Lying in the bath with the water lapping his chin he made up his mind that one day he was going to run away from all this. No houses, no streets, no schools and no stupid people. Instead, he was going to live in a tent somewhere near a lake and a big forest all alone with Mr Bell.

Things seemed a little better next morning, and it was hard not to giggle at the sight of Humphrey staggering drunkenly across the floor with wide-spaced legs and an expression of fierce triumph in his eyes.

'Will he always walk like that? If he does, everyone'll laugh.'

'No, of course not. He only took his first steps a couple of days ago. By the way, have you been up to see Granny yet?'

This was the moment he had been dreading. 'No.'

'She's longing to see you. And Auntie Bella's there, too.'

'Who's Auntie Bella?'

'She's Granny's sister. She's longing to see

you as well.'

'Oh. Yes...'

'And have you thought what you'd like to buy for Granny's birthday present?'

He mumbled that he hadn't, so Willow gave him two pounds from her housekeeping purse and told him to get either bath salts or talcum powder.

'Shall I go now?'

'Yes. Why not?' She looked at him impatiently. 'Go down to the chemist in Bridge Road and don't forget to use the pedestrian crossing.'

The chestnut trees lining the road were looking dark and exhausted now that the end of summer was approaching. He paused outside Alastair's gateway for a moment or two, but apart from the dog barking in the back garden there was no sign of life.

He walked on, and the crackle of the two pound notes in his hand forced him to think about his grandmother.

Now that he didn't like her any more he didn't want to see her, and he certainly didn't want to buy her a present. But he was no longer certain that he wanted her to be dead, either. At camp, and with Mr Bell, the idea had been easy to assimilate, and pride in being entrusted with such a momentous task had outweighed every other consideration. But now, he couldn't help wishing that she would just go away, although that wouldn't really solve the problem either. On Saturday she would be officially declared old, and Mr Bell was quite right when he said that old people shouldn't hog the little bit of space we'd got left after motorways and airports and things had already taken up so much of it. He watched an old lady and an old gentleman strolling arm-in-arm along the opposite pavement and his eyes hardened with dislike.

Mr Bell had said that putting them to sleep was the kindest thing for everybody, and had promised on his honour that the pill they had to swallow didn't cause them any pain.

There was a friendly white-coated woman in the chemist's shop who noticed Oliver hovering by the weighing machine. She asked if she could help him.

He told her that he wanted some talcum powder or some bath salts, and when she asked if it was a present for someone he said Yes, it was.

Because the shop wasn't busy she took a lot of trouble, bringing out box after box and tin after tin, and whenever possible taking the lid off so that he could smell the contents. He dithered helplessly, then after asking how much money he wished to spend, she suggested that he should go for a presentation box which contained a small amount of both bath salts and talc.

'*Muguet*,' she said. 'Which is French for

lilies of the valley.'

He took her advice, feeling relieved that the transaction was almost completed, and was standing by the counter holding the box in both hands when someone touched him lightly on the shoulder.

'Good morning, Oliver.'

He spun round. It was Mr Bell.

'Glad to be home again?' His smile was friendly, yet brisk and businesslike. He was wearing a cream jacket and brown trousers.

'I– Well, I...'

Overcome at seeing him unexpectedly, Oliver could think of nothing to say. Then confusedly aware that Mr Bell's sharp eyes had spotted the fancy box he was holding, tried to hide it down by his side.

'Buying a present? Jolly good.'

'Yes.'

The woman assistant was waiting to take it so that she could wrap it up. She was smiling, and listening to what they were saying.

'I expect it's for your grandmother's birthday, isn't it?'

Crimson with worry and shame, Oliver nodded. He gave the box to the assistant.

'My mother said I'd better – I mean, I thought...'

He didn't know what he thought. He just stood there becoming more and more aware of the dilemma of being caught by Mr Bell of all people in the treasonable act of buying a present for his grandmother. His ears blazed and his tongue swept backwards and forwards across his dry lips.

But Mr Bell didn't seem at all disturbed. He smiled again, and out of the confusion of feelings it suddenly occurred to Oliver that beneath his calm exterior he might be feeling equally embarrassed, for it was quite possible that he had come to buy the pill for his grandmother's Big Goodnight.

Anxious to avoid further mortification for both of them Oliver grabbed the paper bag from the assistant, mumbled goodbye to Mr Bell and made a rush for the door. He was halfway through it when the assistant called him back: 'You've forgotten your change, sonny–'

He returned reluctantly, and was just in time to see Mr Bell paying for a tube of toothpaste.

Outside the shop they stood by the bicycle that was propped against the kerb.

'And when is your grandmother's birthday?'

'Sunday.'

'That's the day after tomorrow.'

'Yes, I know.'

They began to walk away, Mr Bell holding the bicycle with one hand. They turned into a quiet road away from the noise of traffic.

'Do you remember what we talked about, Oliver?'

'Yes.' There was no need to ask when or where.

'Are you still game?'

Mr Bell's pleasantly equable tone belied any hint of doubt or indecision. He might have been speaking about a Young Citizens' sports fixture. Once again Oliver felt his own reservations dwindling and disappearing.

'What'll I have to do?'

'I've told you, it's just a pill that will send her gently to sleep. She won't feel anything at all, she'll just drift off to the Land of Nod as usual, but in the morning she won't wake up. That's all there is to it.'

'Yes.'

'Look at me, Oliver.'

Oliver did so, his gaze sliding up from the warm pavement until it reached Mr Bell's face. His pale eyes were very intent, and Oliver noticed for the first time that they were fringed by short golden lashes that curled outwards.

'You trust me to tell the truth, don't you, Oliver?'

'Yes.'

'It won't hurt. There'll be no pain.'

'No.'

'And I trust you. I trust you absolutely not to tell anyone.'

'I promise I won't.' He couldn't look away. He didn't want to. He just wanted to go on standing there staring up at Mr Bell and thinking that he wanted to be just like him. The love he felt for Mr Bell was unlike anything he had ever known before.

'I promise I won't tell anyone about it,' he said earnestly. 'If they found out and they killed you like you said, I'd–'

'You'd what?'

'I – I don't know.' The idea of a world without Mr Bell was beyond his imagination; he only knew that it would be unbearably awful.

'They won't kill me unless you give the game away,' Mr Bell said. 'And the best way to make sure you don't is just not to say anything. Don't say anything to anyone, especially after your grandmother's – gone to sleep. If you do, it's more than likely they'll kill us both.'

'Both of us?'

'Yes. But I'm sure it won't come to that.' They walked a little further down the road. Apart from a cat sitting on a gatepost it was deserted. 'Now listen, Oliver, it's time to get ourselves organised. Do you know where I live?'

Mr Bell paused again and the cat sat watching them with interest. In appearance it was not unlike Elderberry.

'Yes. Over Krasnor's the jeweller's.'

'Right. Now, if you call round tomorrow evening at about six o'clock – come round the back way and ask for me – I'll give you the pill. I'll seal it up very carefully for you, and it goes without saying that you won't show it to anyone or tell anyone that you've got it. It also goes without saying that you'll be very careful not to lose it – don't even handle it until you come to the right moment to use it. Have you got that?'

Oliver nodded, sweeping his tongue across his top lip.

'Good. Now listen very carefully. The pill will dissolve in water or in any other sort of drink, so I suggest that when Sunday comes you take your grandmother the very nice present you've bought her – is she having a little tea party, by the way?'

'Sort of. But it's at lunchtime and they'll be having wine and stuff.'

A faint quiver of distaste touched Mr Bell's lips. 'Will there be many people there?'

'I don't know.'

'Never mind. It'll be easier for you if she's busy talking to other people. Just watch for the right opportunity, then drop the pill in her glass and that's all there is to it. Any questions?'

There were dozens, but he couldn't disentangle one from another. Finally he said: 'How will the pill know not to work until she goes to bed at night?'

'Because it's a very rare, special one.'

'Where d'you get it from?'

'I had to send away for it.'

'Have you got it yet?'

'No. It's coming.'

Oliver finally removed his gaze from Mr Bell and stood staring at the cat instead. He pictured the pill, small, white and deadly, already making its way silently through the post with all the other letters and bills. He had the fatalistic feeling that it would find his grandmother, unerring as a bullet, without any assistance from him.

'Anything else you want to know?'

Once again he met Mr Bell's eyes while he tried to form another question, but the thoughts as well as the words seemed to have left him. His head was ringing with emptiness.

'Will it fizz?' he managed finally.

'The pill? No.'

They walked to the end of the road in silence, Oliver shifting his grandmother's birthday present from the crook of one arm to the other.

'Now, you've got it quite clear, haven't you?' Mr Bell said as they prepared to part. 'You come to my place tomorrow evening at six for the pill, you keep it very carefully until the next day, then you wait for a suitable moment to drop it into your grandmother's cup – or glass – without anyone seeing, and that's all there is to it.'

'Yes.'

'And you will have saved her from all the misery and pain of old age, as well as helped to provide a little more of the earth's resources for the young people who really need them.'

'Yes.'

Mr Bell placed his hand on top of Oliver's head, tilting it so that once again their eyes met.

'You're a crusader,' he said quietly. 'You belong to a group of very special and very brave people who are fighting for a noble cause. And when you've done what you've promised to do, there'll be another very special secret between us.'

'Oh?' Oliver was too mesmerised even to blink.

'Yes. Everyone else will think that you're just an ordinary little boy, but I'll know the truth. I'll know that you're already a man.'

Abruptly Mr Bell removed his hand from the top of Oliver's head and mounted his bicycle. Turning in a graceful arc he rode swiftly back the way they had come.

Mrs Frewin was enjoying her visit to her sister, but there were one or two things she found a little strange. One of them was Celia's attitude towards Willow.

Willow had always been a funny sort of girl – she didn't start her periods until she was fourteen – and although she was very kind and very clever, she was also very chill. She never really laughed. And Celia, Mrs

Frewin noticed, never seemed to laugh in her presence.

In spite of their professed intimacy there was an air of constraint which seemed to touch Celia's relationship with Seth as well. He too was extremely agreeable whenever they met, but so far they appeared to meet seldom. Mrs Frewin had at first been confident of an invitation to supper over at the main house, but so far none had been issued and in three days' time she was due to return home.

And then Oliver; perhaps he was the strangest of all. She had only caught two glimpses of him since he came back from his mysterious scout-thing. One from the window looking down into the courtyard, and another as a flash of blue jeans and tee-shirt shot out through the gateway as she and Celia were driving in. She remembered how Celia had waved, then pretended to be smoothing her hair when the greeting was ignored. And she spoke of him so proudly, so lovingly, that it only made Oliver's behaviour the more reprehensible. Mrs Frewin wondered whether perhaps he was a little backward.

But during the afternoon of that Friday Mrs Dansie came upstairs with some wild grasses from the garden and said: 'I've just seen Oliver and he's coming up to see us!' Her face was flushed and her voice had a slight tremble.

'Big deal,' said Mrs Frewin laconically. Then repenting, added: 'It'll be lovely to meet him at last.'

'I generally bake some special little cakes for him, but as he's been away I've got out of the habit.'

'Too much sweet stuff is bad for children.'

'These are mainly coconut.' Hastily arranging the grasses in a big stone jug, Mrs Dansie dumped it on the windowledge and then went through to the kitchen. Mrs Frewin heard the sound of teacups clinking.

'We're almost out of orange juice.'

'Won't he drink milk?'

'I ought to have got some tins of coke. I do hope chocolate biscuits will be enough–'

'For God's sake Celia, stop behaving like a nervous virgin!'

'Who – *me?*' Mrs Dansie's head reappeared round the doorway. Indignation gave way to a happy giggle. 'Ah go on, you're only jealous.'

'My turn will come,' Mrs Frewin said sedately. She picked up a magazine and pretended to study it. 'But quite seriously, you do think he's the most marvellous thing walking the earth, don't you?'

'What makes you say that?'

'Oh, just a series of impressions. And how you look when you talk about him.'

Mrs Dansie carried in the tea tray. 'I'm

very fond of him, certainly but I'm also perfectly aware that he's just a normal, ordinary
little boy like any other. Not any cleverer or
better-looking or–'

'Oh, come off it, Celia. Adoration shines
in your eyes like jam.'

'*Jam?*'

'Yes. Stickily.'

Mrs Dansie's retort was silenced by the
sound of footsteps on the stairs. They were
very slow.

'Come in, Oliver!'

He sidled round the door without touching it, then stood looking down at the toes
of his shoes. 'Hullo.'

'Nice to see you after all this time.' Mind-
ful of her sister's ridicule Mrs Dansie strove
to sound offhand. 'By the way, this is Auntie
Bella.'

'Hullo.' He raised his eyes sufficiently to
see her outstretched hand. He took it, then
unobtrusively wiped his fingers on the seat
of his jeans.

'Stay and talk to her while I make the tea.'
Mrs Dansie hastened back to the kitchen.
'I've got some chocolate biscuits, Oliver, but
I haven't got round to making any coconut
pyramids.'

What on earth's the *matter* with Celia?
wondered Mrs Frewin. Anyone would think
she was frightened of him. Smiling at Oliver,
she patted the low stool in front of her.

'Now, come and tell me all about going to camp. I gather you enjoyed it.'

'Yes.' He sat down obediently. 'I want to go back.'

'Well, I expect you will next year, won't you?'

'I want to go back before then.' He raised his head and looked her in the face for the first time she saw a nice-looking child with a tanned skin and large, very white front teeth, but there was an evasive expression in his eyes that disconcerted her. And it was not easy to disconcert Mrs Frewin.

'Are you looking forward to the party on Sunday?'

'Uh-huh.'

'Is Humphrey coming too?'

''Spect so.'

'He's getting quite a big boy now, isn't he? Although I daresay you find people of that age a bit of a drag don't you?'

'He's okay.'

Mrs Frewin sighed inwardly. Her daughter Betsy had been a skilled player of conversational ball from a very early age and sometimes it was difficult to remember that all children were not the same. Oliver sat fiddling with his shoelace.

'Here we are!' cried Mrs Dansie, sweeping into the room with the teapot. She set it down on the tray.

'Glass of milk, Oliver?'

'No thank you.'

'I'm afraid there's only a tiny drop of orange juice–'

'I'm not thirsty.'

'Have a biscuit.'

He took one unwillingly, and began to nibble round the edges. Crumbs fell down his tee-shirt and he brushed them onto the carpet. Mrs Frewin's lips tightened.

Sipping her tea she listened to her sister's attempts to make conversation, and grew increasingly irritated by her attitude towards him which she considered ingratiating to the point of self-abasement.

'It's jolly nice to have you back, Oliver.'

'Uh-huh.'

'What sort of things did you do at camp?'

'Lots of things.'

'Such as?'

'Swam. Went for walks.'

'Tell me more about it.'

'Not much to tell.'

Transferring her gaze from Oliver's bent head and nervously twiddling fingers to her sister, Mrs Frewin's sense of irritation wavered at the hurt look in her eyes. Poor old Celia! Of course she had wanted to show him off to a supposedly jealous non-grandmother, and the little wretch was deliberately making a fool of her. Yet there was more to it than that; more than just a precocious child playing mean with a doting adult, and she became increasingly aware that the constraint between the two of them had a strangely unpleasant undertone. The warm summer air seemed to have become charged with menace, almost as if another presence was lurking unseen and malevolent in the corner.

She put down her cup and saucer with a small crash. 'I've got a headache. I think I'll go and lie down.'

'Oh, Bella...'

Evidently regarding her words as a welcome sign of release Oliver leaped to his feet and sped towards the stair door.

'I've got to go now,' he said, and within the space of two seconds had bolted from view.

'*Well.*' Mrs Frewin stood poised, one hand on the back of her chair.

'He's not a bit like this normally,' Mrs Dansie said bleakly. 'I've obviously done something wrong.'

Concern made Mrs Frewin speak harshly. 'All that's wrong, my dear Celia, is that Willow is too busy to teach him any manners.'

She marched from the room, cursing herself for being cruel and insensitive and probably unwise.

Amory Bell had been intimately acquainted with every nook and cranny of the Krasnors' premises since he first went to live there, exploring the rooms and passages and then the shop itself after the owners were in bed and asleep.

He had stood in their living-room in a pool of torchlight, breathing in the heavy scent of goulash and lace curtains, with his hand resting on the television set still faintly warm from the late night movie. He knew which newspapers they read, he knew the contents of the letters they received, but most of all he knew his way round the small cluttered shop where Papa Krasnor mended watches, re-set stones in rings and cleaned the brooches, baubles and bibelots of his local clientele.

Once he had recovered from the lonely horrors following his grandmother's death he found that he enjoyed the dark, and the sense of being the only person cleanly alert in a world pulsating with snores and the other, grosser acts that took place in the secrecy of bed. He also enjoyed his own stealthiness; the smooth co-ordination of gliding feet with perfect memory for squeaking boards and creaking doors. Sometimes he would sit in one of their easy chairs, in total darkness, for as long as an hour and be mildly amused by the thought of their ignorance next day.

But there was a specific reason for his presence in the shop during the early hours of Saturday morning.

Carefully picking his way behind the counter he went through the doorway that led to the cluttered little workshop. The bench was littered with small tools and disembowelled clocks that glimmered in his carefully screened torchlight and he heard the rapid scutter of a mouse over the bare floor.

At the back of the bench were rows of shelves containing old tobacco tins full of tiny screws and clips, springs and pins, but his hand went unerringly to a square cardboard box with a deep lid. He took it down, opened it and stood looking at the small screw-topped jar inside. He had first read of its contents in Martindale's *Pharmacopoeia* and knew that one of its more innocent uses was for cleaning jewellery.

Holding open a small plastic envelope he had removed from his pocket, he gently tipped a very small amount of white powder from the jar into it. He held his breath until he had replaced the screw top and refolded the plastic envelope. He replaced the box on the shelf and unhurriedly withdrew, his footsteps silent as death itself.

Upstairs in his room he drew the curtains, switched on the light and then went into the small kitchen area. Heating some water in the electric kettle he took a packet of gelatine from his food cupboard and poured a few of the crystals into a cup. The drops of warm water melted them but he continued to stir them briskly, and when the cup had grown cold added the white powder he had taken from the workroom downstairs. Carefully removing the deposit from the bottom of the cup he moulded it between finger and thumb and then coated it with glucose which, like the gelatine, had been purchased specially for the occasion. The finished object, like a small white pea, he held on the palm of his hand while he considered its potential.

This was the first time that he had ever used a poison, and the first time he had ever contemplated using an intermediary as young as Oliver Mitchell, but he knew instinctively that it was going to be a success. The silent work of which he had been sole instigator was now spreading from the London area out into East Anglia, up into the Midlands and even to the West Country, each incident being planned and then put into execution with a smooth professional skill that pleased and satisfied him.

He had always told himself that he was looking forward to the day when he could move into the open; when the more ortho-dox conservationists would have paved the way for a general acceptance of self-destruction at the onset of old age and there would be no further need for the secret work of the Young Fighting Citizens, but of course it was essential to remain patient. At least, things were not stagnating. Even so, he had for some time been aware of a steadily increasing desire to arrange the death of some old person known to him personally. While having no intention of staining his own hands, he was becoming obsessed by the terrible pleasure of murder.

He thought of the Krasnors. And then of the old man who was constantly asking him round to mend a fuse or to sort out his television set; the old man with his ill-fitting teeth and watery shellfish eyes was a constant source of exasperation and would obviously be better off dead.

But then came the evening when Oliver Mitchell brought his grandmother to the concert. Nicely dressed and calmly self-assured, her smiling benevolence had immediately riled him. He had felt his lips tightening, his smile turning to vinegar. He had been unable to sleep because of her that night. Whether his eyes were open or closed he saw her lively intelligent face crowned by the curly white hair so different from his own grandmother's lank, rough-cut locks, and by first light had decided that the Krasnors and the other old man would have to wait a little longer.

His arrangement with young Oliver was of such brilliant simplicity that every now and then he paused to consider whether he could possibly be losing touch with reality a little, but he knew that this was not so. Every aspect of his existence was orderly, sensible

217

and essentially practical, and he was unlikely to act out of character when it came to a matter of such importance. On the contrary, it was becoming increasingly difficult to resist a small jubilant bubble of self-esteem, a growing sense of his own omnipotence.

With a pleasant little smile Amory tipped the pill into another small plastic envelope, folded it tightly, secured it with Sellotape and tucked it away in a drawer.

He washed the cup and spoon with the utmost care, pushed the envelope that had contained the powder into the packet of gelatine, which together with the glucose he left on his table ready for disposal in a public litter bin next morning.

He scrubbed his hands twice before washing his face and cleaning his teeth. He undressed slowly, and went to bed with the words from the Young Citizens' manifesto singing psalmlike in his head. *We believe in the beauty of life; and when it draws towards its natural close we will relinquish it with grace...*

Knowing that righteousness was his he slept well, and during the course of Saturday morning applied himself to his job with customary zeal. The shop in which he worked closed at one o'clock for the weekend and he left promptly for home, skilfully avoiding Mrs Krasnor, who was lying in wait for him with a slice of chocolate *torte*, and gaining the sanctuary of his own room, where he heated a bowl of soup. Oliver was due to arrive at six o'clock to collect the pill and he looked forward to his visit in the way that one looks forward to the successful conclusion of any modest transaction. His unerring knowledge of little boys told him that Oliver would arrive promptly, and that he would come alone, without telling anyone.

But it was only a little after three when a hurried tap sounded at his door. Gliding quietly across the room he opened it, and found himself staring into the eyes of Oliver's grandmother.

'Mr Bell? I'm so sorry to bother you, but I wonder whether you could spare me a few minutes.'

She looked pink and flustered, and his first thought was that something had happened to Oliver which would prevent his calling at six o'clock. With tightly-controlled features he stood aside for her to enter.

'I very much want to have a word with you about Oliver because I'm worried about him and I know that you're an important person in his life, and so I thought perhaps...' She stood in the middle of his room twisting her hands. He sensed that she might be close to tears.

'You thought perhaps, what?' Assured now that nothing was seriously wrong he spoke quite courteously, but he didn't ask her to sit down. He gave her no help whatever.

'I thought perhaps you could give me some advice.'

'About Oliver?'

'Yes. Or at least, let me have your opinion about the extraordinary change in his behaviour. You see, we used to get on so well together – by that I mean that we were good friends in a casual undemonstrative sort of way – but now he's become so different.'

'How?' Pale-eyed and impassive, he stood watching her.

Mrs Dansie looked down at her fingers for a moment, then said in a little choked voice: 'I think he hates me.'

'Why should he do that?'

'I don't know.'

She looked as if she wanted to say more; a lot more. He could imagine with what relief she would sink down in his armchair, accept a cup of tea, possibly even a cigarette, and let all her feelings pour out in a torrent of words. The smiling self-assurance she had exhibited at the concert was nowhere to be seen now, and although her troubles were no concern of his he didn't want her raising last-minute emotional storms in the Mitchell family. Oliver was only a little boy, protected by a little boy's instinctive dislike of mawkish effusion, but it would be dangerous to credit him with the disciplined resistance of an older person; there was always the chance that grandmotherly tears might divert him from the mission entrusted to him.

'I'd help you if I could,' he said finally. 'But as I only see Oliver once a week–'

'You saw him every day for two weeks when he was at camp.'

'Does the change in his attitude date from then?' he asked quickly.

She stood pondering. 'No, a little before. But he's certainly been much more, well – hostile since he came back.'

'And is he hostile towards the rest of the family as well?'

She had to confess that she didn't really know. Watching her, he was certain that she was feeling stupid and wishing that she hadn't come.

'Well, I'm very sorry to hear about this, Mrs er–'

'Dansie. Celia Dansie.'

'Mrs er Dansie. Perhaps you'd like me to have a word with Oliver?'

'Oh no, please don't do that,' she said hastily. 'It's very kind of you, but I think it might make things worse.'

'Boys are funny creatures,' he said. 'Sometimes you think you know them very well, then something happens to make you realise that you don't know them at all. From what I remember, Oliver behaved well at camp. He joined in most of the activities and seemed keen to be associated with the main aims and ideals of our organisation.'

'Yes, I'm sure. He's a very nice child.'

And yes, she did yearn to say more. To sit down and confide in this quiet watchful man all the half-glimpsed, irrational fears that preoccupied her by day and picked holes in her sleep at night. But although she found him more sympathetic than she had expected, she couldn't talk to him any more than she could discuss the subject of Oliver with either his parents or her own sister. She couldn't talk to anyone, she now realised. Loyalty, lack of certainty, and perhaps above all the ignominious fear of being laughed at prevented her from saying *I think my grandson wants me dead.*

So she squared her shoulders and attempted a brave smile, unaware that Mr Bell had been following her line of thought with deadly accuracy.

'I'm sorry about the intrusion.' She turned towards the door. 'It was just a sudden impulse.'

'No trouble.' This time he smiled at her properly, showing small, evenly spaced teeth. 'And I'm sorry I can't help. But perhaps while you're here you wouldn't mind giving Oliver something for me.'

'No, of course not.'

She waited, hands hanging limply at her sides as he moved across the room. A small stack of duplicated pamphlets stood on the table.

'Our quarterly bulletin,' he said. 'It gives a list of Young Citizen activities between now and Christmas.'

'When do the weekly meetings start again?'

'In two weeks' time.'

He rolled the pamphlet into a thin tube then went to the drawer for the Sellotape. He secured it, then with his back towards her deftly inserted the envelope containing the pill into the centre of it. It fitted tightly.

'Thank you very much, Mrs Dansie,' he said, handing it to her. 'It's a great help to us to save postage.'

He glanced at his watch, then walked past her to open the door.

She went meekly, this nicely dressed, self-assured grandmother, and just for a moment or two the poor thing didn't even seem worth hating.

During the course of Saturday morning Oliver had called twice at Alastair's house, only to be told by his mother that he had gone out with his aunty. She hadn't asked him in, and on the second occasion had even told him irritably to buzz off.

So he wandered home again, and spent some of the afternoon sitting high up in one of the trees at the bottom of the garden. Nothing was happening. Nothing was moving. The listless leaves hung like little green rags and even the plum-coloured cloud above them looked as if it had been painted on its blue background.

And he too was suspended in time. Dangling like an insect on a thread between the old innocent days and the dark responsibility of tomorrow.

He had been thinking about it a lot; wondering what would happen when his grandmother didn't wake up on Monday morning, and wondering what they would say when they discovered that she was dead. For his part, he could only really imagine human beings being dead of gunshot wounds during TV car chases. He wondered whether his parents would cry. He knew that he personally wouldn't, although it was possible that he might feel a bit sad, the way the vet was supposed to have done when he did the Big Goodnight on poor Elderberry. Anyway, however he felt, after tomorrow he was going to be a kind of secret grown up because Mr Bell had said so.

Folded in the fork of two branches, he cradled the back of his head against linked fingers while he counted the hours before he went to see Mr Bell. He was due there at six. He wanted to go very much, and to stay for as long as possible, sipping Mr Bell's wisdom and trying to emulate his unique branch of unobtrusive splendour.

He climbed down from the tree in order to

find out the time, planning to glance through the window at the kitchen clock without anyone seeing him. Already he had become an outcast. He hoped that it might be as late as five o'clock, in which case he planned to spend the next half hour washing himself and brushing his hair and cleaning his shoes, and the half hour after that in a calm and leisurely stroll down to the old jeweller's shop and Mr Bell's room above it.

But it was only ten to four. Disheartened he turned away, then deciding to walk down to the river, slipped out of the front gateway and in doing so cannoned into his grandmother. He heard her yelp as he trod on her foot.

'Sorry.' Hastily he prepared to retreat, then stopped abruptly when she spoke his name.

'*Oliver!*' the word was filled with a harsh forcefulness that didn't seem to belong to her.

'Yes?' He hovered uneasily.

'Oliver, I want to speak to you.'

The hand on his shoulder felt very heavy as it propelled him out of the gateway and down the deserted road. He could hear her breathing.

'Now listen, Oliver, I want to know what's wrong.'

'Nothing.' He watched the scuffed toes of his shoes as he walked.

'Then why are you avoiding me?'

'I'm not.'

'Yes, you are.' The hand on his shoulder brought him to a halt and then wheeled him round. They were standing by a low brick wall.

'Oliver, there's something wrong and I intend to find out what it is. You never come to see me, you look furtive whenever we meet, you didn't send me a postcard from camp and before that – on the day the cat was put to sleep – you blurted out that you hated me. I want to know why.'

He didn't say anything.

'Look at me, Oliver. Look me in the face.'

Very unwillingly he raised his eyes. The hand that had been on his shoulders became transferred to his chin, holding it rigid and preventing him from turning his head away.

'Now, tell me what's wrong.'

'Nothing.' His voice rose a little, in protest.

'So do I conclude that you're sulking about nothing?'

She had never talked to him like this before. Riled by the word sulking, he tried to shake his chin free of her hand but it remained there, keeping his jaw rigid and making his words sound slurred and indistinct.

'I'm not sulking.'

'Well, whatever you're doing, I'm getting pretty fed up with it. I've never had much time for bad-mannered people, and if you're going to turn into one you may as well tell me here and now and we can just forget all about being friends.'

But he was staring openly into her face now, unencumbered by embarrassment or fear. In fact, during the time she had been speaking he had suddenly become capable of studying her quite coldly and deliberately, feature by feature. He saw that beneath her old woman's white hair her eyes were angry, that her mouth had a little smudge of pink lipstick in the lined corner of it, and that there was a whisker sprouting on her cheek. He saw that she was angry and ugly and old, and he saw for the very first time through his own eyes that old people didn't deserve to live.

'Oliver...'

Dazzled by the power of this new full-fledged awareness, he was unable to recognise the hurt pleading. With both hands he wrenched his chin free from her grasp and had begun to retrace his steps for home when she called out: 'Here, you'd better have this.'

He heard a light thud behind him, and turning round saw a white rolled up tube of paper lying on the pavement between them.

'It's something from your Mr Bell.'

If she hadn't mentioned Mr Bell he would have left it lying there. Instead, he retraced his steps and picked it up before walking away from her, rigid with the knowledge that he had grown up twenty-four hours ahead of schedule.

The long day died. Shops closed, pubs opened, and ignoring the orange glow of outer London the evening star appeared, bright as a diamond.

Mrs Krasnor set the table for supper while her husband clipped the old wooden shutter over the shop window and reversed the cardboard sign on the door from Open to Closed. He went through to the living-room to find his slippers.

'Have you heard our young man go out?'

'No. He keeps in his room.'

'Without the light?'

'Sometimes he likes to sit without the light to rest his eyes.'

'Ach, that poor young man of ours. He works too hard...'

A last gleam of daylight illuminated the allotments as Seth shouldered the big box of salad stuff that Willow needed for the buffet lunch tomorrow. The thought of tomorrow pleased him. Granny was a dear old thing, and it was important that the boys should grow up in an atmosphere of loving concern that occasionally expressed itself in the form of a small family celebration. He made for the car and home.

'Ham on the bone,' Willow said. 'And I've already done the brown rice salad.'

'Looks delicious.' He kissed her, then put the box of vegetables on the table. 'Boys in bed?'

'Humphrey is. Oliver's gone up but I told him he could read for a while.'

Upstairs in his room Oliver was lying on the bed with the sealed plastic envelope containing the pill resting lightly on his chest. So far he had resisted the temptation to open it. He was thinking about Mr Bell, and wondering if Mr Bell was thinking about him.

To begin with he had been painfully disappointed that Mr Bell had sent the pill via a third person as an obvious indication that he no longer wanted to see him at six o'clock. The fact that the third person was the proposed victim made no difference. He had made up his mind that he would go anyway, until it occurred to him that the less he saw of Mr Bell the better. *If they found out they would kill me*, he had said. *In fact, they might well kill us both* ... or words to that effect. So he changed his mind, and it was some while before he started wondering how Mr Bell had come to meet up with his grandmother.

'Don't forget it's Granny's birthday tomorrow,' Willow had said as she washed his hair in the bath.

He shook his head.

'Daddy and I have made a nice little lunch and we're all going up to her flat at midday. Alastair's coming with his mother and father which will be fun, won't it?'

'Is his auntie coming too?'

'I don't know anything about an auntie,' Willow said, sweeping him with the warm spray. 'Is your red check shirt clean?'

Drowningly he nodded.

'Wear it with your new blue jeans. They're in the airing cupboard next to the sheets.'

He had supper in his dressing-gown, and when his mother asked if he would like to see the present she and Daddy had bought for Granny, he said No.

'Little boys are such funny, private creatures,' Willow said, recounting this to Seth. 'In some ways they're so hard and matter-of-fact, in others so desperately sensitive.'

Oliver's room was almost completely dark when he tucked the plastic envelope under his pillow and fell deeply asleep.

In the granny flat with the satin-stripe wallpaper Mrs Portman-Ayres signed the gift tag in a flourish of green ink and attached it to Mrs Dansie's gift-wrapped biography of Mozart. She placed it on the hall table in readiness for the next day, then went through to the bedroom to pin up her hair and manicure her nails.

She had no idea of the kind of circles Celia Dansie moved in, or who would be attending her birthday luncheon, but had every intention of being the most impressive woman there.

The evening star was already fading.

'Do we really have to go?'

'Well, I'm going. You can please yourself.'

'But it's not as if she's a friend, is it?'

'She is a friend of sorts. But as I said, you can please yourself.'

'What about Alastair?'

'Well, what about him?'

Down the road from the Mitchells' house, Alastair's parents confronted one another in the harsh light of the garage. Love had fled, and the strain of being unable to argue without being overheard and remonstrated with by auntie was becoming intolerable.

'You'd better come,' Alastair's mother said finally. 'After all, it'll be for the last time, won't it?'

A black sky now, and trees rustling overhead.

Mrs Dansie lay listening to the comfortable snores coming from her sister's room and mourned the fact that she had made a fool of herself twice in one day. The impulse that had driven her to seek advice from Mr Bell had been as hopelessly misguided as the way in which she had handled her encounter with Oliver. And it was no use telling herself that she could retrieve the situation tomorrow, because she still didn't know what the situation was.

Tomorrow. Tomorrow she would be officially declared old; in her new role as pensioner she would be entitled to free passes on the local buses and would no longer have to pay public library fines. There were probably other things too, but none of them would compensate for the knot of foreboding that seemed to be pulling her nerves tighter and tighter. Irritably she turned on her side, but it was a long while before sleep came.

The streets were very quiet now. Only the sound of a police siren wailing somewhere far away.

Upstairs in his room Amory Bell sat in the dark, fully-dressed. Night-loving as a spider, he was able to remain awake without effort on this eve of yet another Big Goodnight. He was keeping a vigil.

Stretching ahead of him was his own new version of this poor distracted and dilapidated planet, graced now by young people of resourceful intelligence who were solemnly aware of the thousand million other forms of life that had had increasingly to struggle to maintain a tenuous foothold on it. In his vision of the future, the delicate hair's-breadth balance of it all had been restored because the human lifespan had been readjusted and there was no longer any sentimental attachment to that which was old, ailing and ugly.

Returning to the present, he remembered the worried elderly woman who had invaded his privacy that afternoon, and who had departed carrying the means of her own destruction with her. Giving her the poison capsule hidden in the roll of paper had been a risky thing to do, and a year ago he would never have dreamed of such a thing. But now, the certainty of his own invulnerability was absolute. There was no question of losing touch with reality, it was merely that his work was being given the personal protection of a grateful God of all the universe. He had a talisman to prove it.

Opening his clenched hand he tilted it towards the window. A faint gleam of light touched the small hard object, like a little pearly stone, that lay on his palm. It was Oliver Mitchell's tooth.

The buffet lunch was set out on the table in the centre of the room and the windows were open onto the balcony. Down in the garden a robin sang with piercing sweetness and Mrs Dansie appeared in the doorway and said to Mrs Frewin; 'Do I really look all right in this dress?'

'Yes, fine.' Mrs Frewin was wearing a silk

skirt, and matching top. 'Your hair looks nice, too.'

'So does yours.'

They surveyed one another very seriously for a moment, both conscious that Mrs Dansie was in the act of passing through some important but invisible time-barrier. So far they hadn't bickered once since waking, and Mrs Dansie had been genuinely delighted by the Victorian enamel trinket box that Mrs Frewin had given her.

'Many, *many* happy returns, Celia dear.' She had kissed her, and said the words slowly, as if they really meant something.

'I always feel nervous before a party.'

'No need to with this one. It's mostly family.'

'Families can make you feel very nervous sometimes.'

For a moment Mrs Frewin was tempted to say that she hoped Oliver's behaviour would have improved. Instead, she remarked that there was a fly buzzing round the cold sausages.

'Well, shoo it off, then.'

'Shooing's a waste of time. Where's the aerosol?'

'You can't spray aerosol among food. You'll poison everyone.'

'Honestly Celia, fancy thinking about death on your birthday!'

Mrs Dansie's smile was bleak, but it

widened to one of genuine pleasure at the sound of voices and footsteps on the stairs.

They all seemed to arrive at once, bringing with them the cheerful rustle of gift paper and a chorus of birthday greetings. Humphrey was lifted up to give her a novice's kiss and Oliver tendered his box of bath salts and talcum powder with a smile that was small but adequate.

Due to a little careful calculation Mrs Portman-Ayres arrived a few minutes later, hesitating in the doorway for a second before advancing with gloved arms outstretched.

'My *dear*...' She brushed Mrs Dansie's cheek with her own and placed in her hands the copy of *Mozart: A Definitive Biography*. 'I have brought you what I hope will prove an entertaining bedfellow on long winter nights.'

Mrs Dansie laughed a shade apprehensively, and felt relieved when Seth began to pour the drinks.

Oliver and Alastair met over by the standard lamp. They hadn't seen one another since their return from camp and the feeling of constraint was increased by very clean clothes and very smoothly brushed hair.

'Knock, knock, who's there?'

'Dunno.'

'Luke.'

'Luke who?'

'Luke through the keyhole and you'll see.'

'Huh. Can we go and play with your Lego?'

235

'No,' said Oliver, aware that here was a hazard he hadn't envisaged. With Alastair in constant attendance, the disposal of the Goodnight pill in his grandmother's glass was not going to be all that easy.

He glanced across at her, and saw that she was holding her glass close to her lips and chatting to his mother over the top of it. Obviously he would have to wait until she put it down.

'Why can't we?'

'Because we're supposed to be *here*.'

'Listen, I've got something to tell you.'

'What?' Oliver looked at Alastair with a certain amount of hostility. He was still a bit fed up with him for never being at home when he called.

'I'm going to live in America with my auntie.'

'Bet you're not.'

'Yes, I am. It's all fixed.'

'Now then, what would you two boys like to drink?' Mrs Frewin bore down on them. 'Orange, lemon, coke?'

They both said they would have coke.

'Right then, Oliver. You can come and fetch it, can't you?'

He followed her across the room and round the buffet table. Humphrey, in little bib-and-brace overalls was sitting on the floor examining the contents of his mother's handbag. Oliver strode over him, then found his way barred by a big old woman with a funny smooth face and long gloves stretching up her arms.

'Are you Oliver?'

He said that he was.

'How do you do, Oliver? My name is Mrs Portman-Ayres and I am a friend of your grandmother.'

Oliver smiled politely. He wanted to move away, but having shaken his hand she was still holding on to it.

'You must find it enormous fun to have her living so close to you. I live very close to my three little grandchildren and they spoil me *terribly*. Every afternoon after school they pop along to my flat and tell me all about their day, and about all the things they've been doing, and sometimes they bring me little things they've made. Lucy, who is only six, has made me the most *marvellous* paper elephant and I keep it on my bedside table so that I can see it the *moment* I wake up.'

He didn't know what to say in return, but suspected that she was one of those grown ups who prefer not to be interrupted. So he waited patiently until she had finished with his hand, and then hurried after his Auntie Bella.

Near the door that led to the stairs Willow and Seth were presenting Mrs Dansie with a large object wrapped in flowery paper.

'Oh, my dears...' She placed her glass on

a nearby bookshelf and began to untie the fastenings. The rustle of paper attracted everyone's attention and they watched, glasses in hand, as Mrs Dansie pulled aside the paper and revealed a shopping trolley. It was very capacious and splendid and shining, with a waterproof cover to fit over the top when it rained.

She thanked them dazedly, and with a crow of delight Humphrey abandoned Willow's handbag and pounded unsteadily across to this glittering new toy.

'We deliberately chose one with four wheels instead of two,' Willow explained, 'because it's more of a support for you when you get tired. Look – let go of it Humphrey, there's a good boy – you can lean on it quite heavily.'

Dismissing an ignoble vision of geriatric walking-frames Mrs Dansie thanked them both very sincerely, admired it lavishly, and then amid laughter scooped up Humphrey and stood him inside it. She pushed him slowly round the room.

Watching, Oliver's fingers crept towards his new jeans pocket and to the pill that was lying in the bottom of it. He was no more than three feet away from his grandmother's glass and now seemed as good a time as any. His heart began to beat very heavily, then his Auntie Bella nudged him with her elbow and said: 'Hey, do you two boys want this or not?'

He took the two glasses of coke from her and carried them over to where Alastair was eating a cheese biscuit.

'It fell off the plate,' he said.

Seth refilled everyone's glass and the conversation became a shade louder.

Alastair's mother moved across to where Willow was replacing the contents of her handbag and said: 'Willow, I've got something to tell you. Peter and I are parting.'

'Oh, *no!*'

''fraid so.'

'Oh Jane, how awful. I mean, is it really final?'

'Yes.' Alastair's mother looked gently sorrowful. 'Quite honestly, it's been trickling to an end for the past two years.'

'And there's absolutely no hope of...?' Willow fastened her handbag and accepted a refill of Evian water from Seth. She smiled at him very brightly.

'None whatever,' Alastair's mother said as Seth moved away, 'although we're determined to keep the drama down to a minimum, of course. Neither of us see any reason why we shouldn't go on being excellent friends – after all, we'll always have Alastair in common–'

'I was just going to ask about Alastair. What's going to happen to him?'

'Well,' Alastair's mother said carefully, 'just to begin with, Peter's elder sister is taking him back to the States with her. I mean, he'll have a marvellous time out there, the Americans are so friendly and so go-ahead–'

'Does Alastair know yet?'

'Oh, yes. We don't believe in keeping anything from him.'

'And what's his reaction?'

'Thrilled to bits. Honestly Willow, if I didn't understand how children's minds work I'd probably felt quite hurt at the way he leaped at the chance.'

'Poor Alastair,' Willow said, then added with swift diplomacy: 'And poor you, too. It must be awful.'

'It is,' Alastair's mother agreed. 'But there you are.'

Normally Seth was not a drinking man, confining himself mostly to a glass of home-brewed beer on a hot day, but when it came to her birthday party his mother-in-law had proved unexpectedly firm at the last minute.

'If you and Willow are providing the food,' she had said, 'then I am providing the drinks, and let there be no argument about substituting good honest alcohol with reinforced turnip juice.'

He hadn't really agreed, but now, after two small whiskies and water, it seemed a good idea. He found himself standing next to Mrs Frewin.

'Hullo, Seth.' Hers was one of those faces

with an acid expression sweetened now and then by a disarming grin. 'Nice party.'

'Seems to be going well, doesn't it? How's your glass?'

'At the moment, there's about three inches to spare at the top.'

'I take the hint.' White teeth showing in a smile, he took her glass over to the drinks table. He refilled his own as well. The noise in the room was now considerable, and on returning he had to lean close to her to make himself heard. His beard tickled her cheek.

'Do you really think Granny's happy here?'

'I'm not sure. What's your opinion?'

Having taken his mother-in-law's happiness as a foregone conclusion the question had been only a rhetorical one, and Seth was nonplussed that Mrs Frewin should sound even mildly uncertain. He swallowed a little more whisky and water.

'All I know is that she's a lovely old lady and that we're very glad to–'

'Sixty isn't old,' Mrs Frewin said. 'She's not ready for the scrap heap yet.'

'Good Lord, no–'

'In fact, Celia's still young and able, with quick wits coupled with wisdom and experience, and they ought to be made more use of.'

Taken aback by her vehemence, he could only ask how.

'That's up to you and Willow. How often

241

does she see you? How often does she see your friends? Has she–'

'Any friends of her own?' Seth indicated Mrs Portman-Ayres, who was now talking to Alastair's father in a series of sweeping gestures. 'I gather that's one of them. And Willow and I have certainly laid down no constriction on Granny's comings and goings, or made any rules about who she makes friends with–'

'But that's not enough!' hissed Mrs Frewin.

'Look at her over there by the window with Oliver and tell me whether their relationship, for instance, needs any additional encouragement.' Slightly miffed, Seth moved away to speak to someone else.

'I was so pleased with my present,' Mrs Dansie was saying. 'Did you buy it yourself?'

'Yes.'

'Every time I use it I'll be able to think of you.'

Oliver smiled, and watched as she placed her glass on the window-ledge. Automatically his hand moved towards his jeans' pocket.

'Alastair's going to live in America.' He hoped she would look across the room at Alastair for a second or two, but she didn't. Instead, she looked with great concern at him. And she didn't seem cross with him like she had been yesterday.

'Oh heavens, is he? Why? Are his parents

moving there?'

'No,' said Oliver, edging a shade closer to the window-ledge. 'He's going to live with his auntie.'

'But why?'

'I don't know.'

'Does he want to?' She seemed genuinely anxious.

'Well, you can't always tell because he swanks so much about everything–'

'You'll miss him, won't you?'

Suddenly aware that this was the nearest approach to a conversation they had had for several weeks, Mrs Dansie picked up her glass and took a happy little sip. But before she had time to swallow it, Oliver had walked away.

He met up with Alastair again.

'Hullo, fat nit.'

'Listen, knock, knock, who's there?'

'Dunno.'

'Arfur.'

'Arfur who?'

'Arfurgot.'

'Huh.' But even so, he began to realise that he would miss Alastair.

They had known one another for a long time, and it was Alastair who had first told him about Big Goodnight. For a moment it was extremely tempting to tell him about what was going to happen very shortly; to confide in him, to swank back at him, and perhaps elicit a little sympathy for the difficulties he was having. It would also be extremely gratifying to show him the pill, the actual Big Goodnight pill which had been entrusted to him by Mr Bell, and to tell him what Mr Bell had said about him really being a grown up.

His fingers slid back into his pocket, then he heard the sharp rattle of plates and the jingle of a trayful of fresh glasses. There was the pop of a cork.

'Golly, they're going to start eating!'

'You've been eating ever since you arrived,' Oliver said sourly.

Down in the depths of his pocket he could feel the pill becoming stuck and a bit misshapen against the sides of its envelope. He hoped that this wouldn't impair its efficiency. Before coming to the party he had opened the envelope in readiness, and now he sauntered towards the buffet table gently massaging its contents back into a ball shape through the layer of plastic. Although it was only a sort of super sleeping pill with a delayed action, he now preferred to think of it in terms of an agreeably dangerous little bomb. If he tripped and fell it would explode, killing him and everyone else in the room.

But make-believe games apart, having missed at least two opportunities with his grandmother's first glass of wine-stuff he would certainly have to do it with her second.

He wished they'd all stop talking and moving about so much.

'Come along, boys!' someone called, holding out two plates. 'Come and help yourselves.'

They did so, spooning up the salads and spearing ham and sausages with their forks. They sat down on the floor.

'Not with your fingers, Alastair!' called Alastair's mother.

'Fingers were made before forks,' quipped Mrs Portman-Ayres, who had now removed her gloves. With a well-stocked plate and a glass of white wine she sailed triumphantly towards an easy chair.

Everyone was sitting down now; sitting, or perching on the arms of chairs while they ate bean sprouts and alfalfa and carrot mousse and cottage cheese with nuts and tomatoes in yogurt dressing, and with a sudden brilliant clarity Oliver saw that the moment had arrived. If it had been engineered by Mr Bell himself, it couldn't have been made easier for him.

His grandmother was sitting in a low chair next to Auntie Bella and close to Alastair's father. They were all talking happily, animatedly, and his grandmother's glass of wine was on a little stool by her side. Twice, while he watched, her hand went out to it, picked it up by its stem and conveyed it to her mouth, then put it down again. She wasn't looking at it. No one was looking at it. They were all too busy eating and talking and looking at each other.

With businesslike zeal Oliver finished what was on his plate before getting up and going back to the buffet for more. Only Alastair watched him dreamily, his mouth stuffed full of home-baked bread.

No one else noticed him. No one made a joke about Oliver Twist, and no one saw the small careful fingers withdraw the pill and drop it so gently that it barely disturbed the surface of the wine in his grandmother's glass. He reached the big table and wiped his hand on the backside of his jeans before composedly helping himself to a little more ham.

'Okay, let's be frank,' Alastair's mother was saying to Willow. 'We've both got someone else. Peter met this girl who's a photographer and one night last winter I met up with a chap I was at college with – when I look back he was just an ordinary sort of chap with big feet and a grin, but now–'

'But now, it's different?' Willow poked fussily at a morsel of shredded cabbage before conveying it to her mouth.

'We can't help ourselves. All we can do is to be honest...'

'To be absolutely honest,' Alastair's father was saying to Mrs Dansie, 'we've reached the parting of the ways. Jane and I are getting a divorce...'

'What about the dog?' Willow was asking Alastair's mother. 'Who's going to take care of the dog?'

Sitting on the floor close to Alastair, Oliver listened to the tide of conversation turning, shifting, rising and falling. He watched his grandmother's hand reach out for her glass. His tongue began to wag backwards and forwards across his top lip and suddenly he couldn't eat any more ham.

'For God's sake, Bella,' Mrs Dansie was saying, 'it was Henry Hall who started the BBC Dance Band.'

'Henry Hall, my foot. It was Billy Cotton.'

'Billy–?' Mrs Dansie's hand lifted the wine glass, held it poised for a moment, then set it down again. 'You must be mad.'

'Henry Hall played strict tempo for ballroom dancing.'

'Henry Hall did *not* play strict tempo, Bella. You're thinking of Victor Sylvester–'

No one saw Humphrey suddenly burst from under the long white tablecloth that covered the buffet table. Looking for some more bean sprouts he set off towards his mother, then abruptly changing course lurched briskly towards the little stool by the side of his grandmother. He reached it, and intrigued by the play of light on the contents of her glass, seized it in both fat little hands and drank the lot.

It took such a pitifully short while, and the convulsions had already begun when they first noticed that something was wrong.

'That child–' cried Mrs Portman-Ayres. 'That poor child is having a fit!'

Willow screamed, and Mrs Dansie fell out of her chair onto her knees. She tried to hold him, to stop the terrible turmoil that was shaking him and transforming him into a choking, tortured marionette. With a strength that didn't belong to him he was arching his body backwards, taut as a sprung bow, then collapsing into a shuddering, juddering little heap. His face, splashed with vomit and froth, was unrecognisable.

'Get a doctor!'

'It's a teething fit–'

'Dial 999 – ambulance–'

Pushing Mrs Dansie aside Seth picked Humphrey up and held him close to his chest.

'Sshh-sshh. There, little baby, all over now…' He enfolded him between chest and arms and bowed head, and Humphrey seemed quieter. The violent agitations that had racked his body and torn off one of his shoes were becoming fainter. He hung limp, and only one foot swung every now and then. Out of the silence came the *ting* of the telephone and the sound of dialling.

'The doctor's coming straight away.'

Willow's voice was shaking and her face very pale. She walked back through the group of motionless, horrified observers and held out her arms to Seth.

'Let me put him on Granny's bed where it's quiet.'

'I'll get a hot water bottle,' Mrs Dansie said, without moving.

Very slowly Seth released his tightly protective embrace and held Humphrey outstretched on his arms.

'His eyes are open,' Willow said wonderingly.

'He's dead. Oh Christ, he's dead.'

No one could move, or speak. Neither could they cry. Only the robin down in the garden continued its bitter-sweet song, and it was not until the doctor formed a tragic little procession to the bedroom with Willow and Seth that life began to creep back into them.

They became aware of one another. Aware of the mess of plates and glasses and crumpled paper napkins. Mrs Dansie's shopping trolley lay abandoned by the buffet table and Humphrey's shoe was resting on the rug where it had fallen. No one touched it. No one touched anything.

It was Alastair suddenly bursting into loud hiccoughing sobs that prompted Mrs Frewin to look around her and say: 'Where's Oliver?'

'I know where he is.'

Mrs Dansie struggled, ungainly for a moment, from the rug where she had knelt with Humphrey. She picked up his shoe, laid it carefully on the small stool that had held her wine-glass, then left the room. After the space of a second or two, no one missed her.

The road was warm and bathed in honey-coloured Sunday sunlight yet her teeth were chattering as she half-ran down towards Bridge Road. It was only two-fifteen and lunchtime drinkers were leaving The Albion, the Red Lion and the Prince of Wales. The smell of roast beef floated from open windows.

Panting, she turned the corner towards the Krasnors' shop, propelled by what seemed like blind instinct rather than any form of reasoning. There was nothing in her mind except images of horror, each one of them seared onto it like a brutal photo-graph. The calm wax features of Mrs Port-man-Ayres flying apart like a shattered plate; the face of young Alastair like a pink balloon with some of the air released, and the quiet private anguish of Seth bending his head low over the body of Humphrey. She wanted to cry, to scream, but all she could do was seize the old-fashioned door knocker of the jeweller's shop and crash it up and down with both hands.

A startled old woman in black opened the door and Mrs Dansie pushed her roughly aside without speaking. She ran down the long dark hallway and up the stairs. Her feet seemed to remember the way of their own accord and the blankness only lifted from her mind when she flung open the door and stood staring at the man sitting in the chair by the window. He had the appearance of someone who was waiting for something.

'Where's Oliver?'

The quick flash of alarm in his eyes instantly confirmed everything.

'Feel as if you're seeing a ghost, Mr Bell?'

'I don't know what you're talking about.' He had risen and came towards her. Alarm had immediately given way to cold dislike.

'Where's Oliver? What have you done with him?'

'What are you imagining I've done with him?'

She grabbed his arm and started shaking it roughly. 'Oliver's missing. Whatever you gave him to put in my drink killed his small brother instead. Oliver watched him die – we all did – and now Oliver's disappeared–'

'I don't understand anything you're saying except that Oliver's disappeared.' Calmly he detached himself from her grasp. 'Please don't touch me, just tell me what makes you think you'll find him here?'

'Because you're responsible for what happened – you're some sort of terrible madman – it all fits in–'

Stumbling across the room she swept aside the plastic curtain that concealed the gas burner and the small sink. She flung open the wardrobe door, breathlessly calling his name.

'Oliver is not here.' Amory spoke loudly and distinctly, as if to a halfwit or a foreigner. 'I have not seen him. But if you are worried that he is missing I will come and help you to find him. Have you rung the police?'

She shook her head, fighting down a huge sob.

Ignoring the two Krasnors, who were standing in silent consternation at the foot of the staircase, they hurried out into the street.

'Have you any idea of the best place to start looking?'

'I don't want you to come–'

'He's probably gone to a friend's house. What about Alastair Grant?' His calmness was extraordinary.

'He's at the party–'

'What about the river? There's some sort of regatta on down there.'

'Go away!' she cried violently. 'I don't want you anywhere *near!*'

'Oh, don't be so stupid,' he said tiredly.

They turned into Bridge Road, Mrs Dansie sobbing openly now and trying to hasten ahead of Amory. He remained by her side, striding smoothly and silently, his face very pale.

The traffic was increasing, the last drinkers leaving the pubs and mingling with the first of the Sunday afternoon trippers when Mrs Dansie saw Oliver through a rainbow of tears.

'There he is!'

He was standing on the opposite pavement, small and pinch-faced and irresolute, his tongue flicking backwards and forwards across his top lip. He saw them, and turned as if to run; then changed his mind and seemed to be on the point of running across the road towards them. His movements were as piteous as those of a little lost dog.

'Oliver!' Mrs Dansie screamed, but the sound was lost in the harsh screech of brakes. She heard rather than saw people running.

'He just walked straight out!'

'He must have seen the van!'

'He saw it, but he didn't seem to take any notice–'

'It was just plain *suicide!*'

Amory Bell lay in the roadway, his pale closed face upturned to the sun. His hair was still neatly in place even as his lifeblood drained away under the front wheels of the Help the Aged minibus. Wrinkled, agitated old faces were peering out of its windows, fearful that whatever had happened would jeopardise their prospects of a cream tea down at the regatta.

Her one thought was to conceal the fact that she was involved. She wanted no help, and above all no kind of inquisitive sympathy. Forcing herself to walk resolutely Mrs Dansie crossed the road away from the accident and found Oliver.

'Come on,' she said, 'we'd better go back.'

He walked with her away from the noise of voices and the wail of an approaching siren. She couldn't see his face but his words were tumbled and distraught. 'He told lies – he told lies! It *did* hurt!'

'Mr Bell's dead.'

'I don't care! What he said was all *lies!*'

'Oliver…' With what seemed like the last of her strength she put her arm round his shoulders but he jerked away from her. And she saw then that his face was bleached white by a new, fanatical hatred.

'Don't touch me,' he said. 'From now on, I don't want anyone touching me again, not ever.'

This Large Print Book, for people
who cannot read normal print,
is published under the auspices of

THE ULVERSCROFT FOUNDATION